"Jak [...] dance the night away at the prom," Christy said to the group, which consisted of her parents and my mom. "It'll be just like a movie," she added.

Then she leaned in close to me. "Just like a *bad* movie," she whispered.

Absurdly, Christy's stinging remark was like getting a knife in the chest. I quickly removed my arm from her shoulders and put my hands in my lap. So much for Ms. Nice Girl. Christy was just being nice to me to please her mother. I should have known.

Yes, I *should* have known. But for that one second, when I had thought that she actually *meant* we were going to dance the night away, my heart had thumped.

You're insane, Jake, I told myself. *You don't even like this girl.*

Do you?

Prom Trilogy

Jake & Christy

ELIZABETH CRAFT

BANTAM BOOKS
NEW YORK · TORONTO · LONDON · SYDNEY · AUCKLAND

For my mom

RL: 6, AGES 012 AND UP

JAKE & CHRISTY
A Bantam Book / April 2000

Cover photography by Michael Segal.

Copyright © 2000 by 17th Street Productions,
an Alloy Online, Inc. company, and Elizabeth Craft.
Cover art copyright © 2000 by 17th Street Productions,
an Alloy Online, Inc. company.

Produced by 17th Street Productions,
an Alloy Online, Inc. company.
33 West 17th Street
New York, NY 10011.

ISBN: 0-553-49320-5

Visit us on the Web! www.randomhouse.com/teens

Published simultaneously in the United States and Canada

Bantam Books is an imprint of Random House Children's Books, a
division of Random House, Inc. BANTAM BOOKS and the rooster
colophon are registered trademarks of Random House, Inc. Bantam Books,
1540 Broadway, New York, New York 10036.

PRINTED IN THE UNITED STATES OF AMERICA

OPM   0 9 8 7 6 5 4 3 2 1

Prologue

The Summer Before Eighth Grade

CHRISTY REDMOND RUBBED her hands against the fabric of her favorite white skirt and hoped that Jake Saunders wouldn't notice how sweaty her palms were. This was the most significant night of her thirteen years on the planet, and she wanted every detail of the evening to be perfect.

So far, so good, Christy thought. Mr. Saunders had dropped them off in the parking lot of the Star Diner, and he hadn't said anything embarrassing about how cute they looked all dressed up or commented in that *parent* voice that they were really "all grown up now." That would have been totally humiliating!

"Ready to go inside?" Jake asked, pulling open the door of the diner.

"Uh, yeah." Duh. Christy wished she had said something clever, but tonight she felt completely tongue-tied.

Usually she felt so comfortable around Jake that he had a hard time shutting her up. But tonight was different. Tonight they were on a *date*. Jake had asked, and Christy had accepted. So even though they'd been buddies forever, even though they'd practically grown up together because their moms were best friends, Christy knew that something had changed between them.

And that something was the fact that friends didn't kiss. But people on dates did.

And for a couple of weeks now, all Christy could think about was what it would be like to kiss Jake Saunders. Her best friend. He must have been feeling the same way since he was the one who asked her out—on a real date.

Her first real date. And so far, it was everything she'd imagined. Everything really was different tonight. Jake even *looked* different. He was wearing khaki pants that she had never seen before and a white, button-down shirt that he had actually bothered to tuck in.

"We'd like a table by the window," Jake informed a waiter as he and Christy walked into the restaurant. "Preferably a booth."

The waiter rolled his eyes. "Do I look like a maitre d', kid? Sit wherever you want. Preferably *not* a booth since it's just the two of you."

Christy cringed. A shot of red crept up Jake's cheeks.

"Does he want a tip?" Jake asked, loudly enough for the waiter to hear him. "Sue me for wanting a nice table."

"Forget him," Christy whispered in Jake's ear. "He probably hates teenagers. Let's just sit down. I see a table over there."

Jake smiled. "Okay."

They sat down at a table for two by the window. A large, green hanging plant was right over Christy's head. *Please don't fall on me,* she prayed as another waiter dropped two menus on the table. *That would be just what I need. A head full of dirt on my first date!*

The waiter returned, snapping open his order pad and removing a short pencil from behind his ear. "What'll it be?"

Christy's mouth was watering. She knew exactly what she wanted: a bacon double cheeseburger, medium rare, well-done fries, some coleslaw, an extra pickle, and a large Coke with a lemon wedge. "I'll have a tossed salad, dressing on the side, and an iced tea, please."

Jake raised an eyebrow. "What else?"

Christy shut her menu. "That's it." She smiled at the waiter, handing her menu to him.

Jake stared at her as if there was something wrong with her, then shrugged and turned his attention to the waiter. He ordered everything Christy had been dreaming of except he got a milk shake instead of a Coke. When the waiter left, Jake said, "You knew we were going to have dinner, so why'd you eat something before?"

Huh? she thought. What was he talking about? "I didn't. I haven't eaten anything since breakfast. Why would you think I did?"

3

"Why else would you order just a salad, then? And since when do you drink iced tea?"

Christy felt herself redden. "I'm just trying to eat lighter these days, that's all." Okay, that was a total lie. But she couldn't eat like a pig in front of Jake. Not tonight anyway. Did he have to make such a big deal about what she ordered?

"So I'm really psyched for the movie we're going to see," she told him, dying to change the subject. Jake's eyes lit up at the mention of the film. They talked excitedly and easily about their expectations of it, and Christy felt herself relax. This was more like it. *This* was a date.

"Yum," Christy said as she saw the waiter headed toward them with their orders. "There's nothing like a crisp, green salad."

Again Jake looked at her like she had two heads. "Usually you eat like there was no tomorrow."

She felt her cheeks flame again and then realized she was more angry than embarrassed. That comment wasn't very nice. Who was he to say anything about how much or how little she ate? *Calm down, Christy,* she told herself. *Guys aren't known for their sensitivity*. Christy decided to let it pass—in the name of love. Besides, she *did* have a tendency to eat a lot.

"Here you go, kiddies," the waiter announced. "One salad, one cheeseburger with the works."

Jake glared at the waiter. "We're not—"

"Going to need anything else, thanks!" Christy cut in brightly. The waiter left, and Christy breathed a sigh of relief. The last thing she needed was for Jake and the guy to get into a fistfight. "Just forget it, okay?" she whispered urgently to Jake. "Don't say anything rude if he comes back with more water or something."

"Why should I let him talk to us that way?" Jake demanded. "Who does he think he is? And he's not that much older than we are. He's like seventeen or something."

"Your fries are getting cold," she told him with a smile. "Let's dig in, okay?"

Jake nodded, grabbing the squirt bottle of ketchup. He turned it upside down over his fries and squeezed, but nothing came out. He shook the bottle, then tried again.

"Do you need help with that?" she asked, reaching for the bottle.

"Nope." Jake shook the bottle vigorously. "I can handle it."

Then he squeezed the bottle, using what looked like all of his upper-body strength. The ketchup shot out of the bottle as if it were coming from an old-fashioned cannon. And it landed all over the pale yellow cotton sweater she had so carefully chosen from her closet less than an hour ago.

"Oh no!" Christy shrieked. "It's all over me."

"Sorry!" Jake turned bright red as he grabbed a fistful of napkins from the dispenser. "Here, let me help you."

But as he leaned across the table with the napkins, his sleeve caught on the straw that was sticking out of his milk shake. In a split second the entire contents of the glass landed on her skirt.

"Jake!" she cried. "I can't believe you! You're such a—"

He froze, napkins in hand. "Such a *what?*"

"Look at me!" she shrieked. "My outfit's completely ruined!"

"I'm *sorry*," he yelled. "Jeez! It was an accident."

Christy grabbed the napkins out of his hand and wiped futilely at her skirt and sweater. This whole date was turning into a disaster. She didn't want to leave the table, much less go to a movie theater looking like this.

She put the wet pile of napkins on the table and glared at Jake. A little while ago she had thought he was the greatest guy in the world. But now . . . he didn't even look cute. Okay, he *did* look cute. But still . . . this date wasn't anything like she'd thought it would be.

Jake stared in horror at the mess he had created. He felt bad about what had happened, but truthfully, it *was* an accident. He hadn't meant to squirt her with ketchup. And as for the milk shake spilling onto her skirt . . . he had just been trying to help!

What was he supposed to do? She was completely freaking out. It wasn't as if she had broken her arm—she just had a little food on her clothes. No biggie.

"Calm down," Jake told her. "Everybody is staring at us."

In particular, Jake had spotted three guys from the eighth grade, sitting at a table on the other side of the diner. They were pointing at Jake and Christy's booth and laughing hysterically.

"Hey, Saunders!" one of them called. "You want one of us to pinch-hit on your date? It doesn't look like you're doing such a great job of it yourself."

Humiliation. Total and utter humiliation. He slid down in the booth, hoping to avoid any further comments from the boys.

"Shut up!" Christy yelled at the guys. "Nobody asked for your opinion!"

They howled. "Oh, she's a blast!" another called.

Could he die now, or would that be too much to ask for? It wasn't like he could challenge them to a fight over Christy's honor. They would kill him! Each one was practically twice his size.

"Why don't we get the check?" Jake asked Christy. "I've suddenly lost my appetite."

She looked up from the fresh bunch of napkins she was using to dab at her sweater. "Good idea," she agreed. "If I don't soak these clothes soon, they'll be ruined forever."

But the waiter was one step ahead of them. Before Jake could even catch his eye, he placed the check in front of him on the table. "I'll take that whenever you're ready, *sir*."

"I'm ready now," Jake responded. He reached into the back pocket of his khakis to get his wallet.

But nothing was there. Quickly he reached into the other pocket. Nothing. No wallet. No money.

7

Just a lint ball from the dryer. Suddenly his face felt like it was on fire. Jake knew exactly where his wallet was. On the top of his dresser, where he had put it just before he slipped into his pants.

"What's wrong?" Christy asked.

Jake took a deep breath. "I forgot my wallet," he whispered, not wanting the waiter to know.

"You forgot it?" she repeated loudly. "Jake!"

"I—I'm sorry," he stammered, for what felt like the hundredth time since their date had begun such a short time ago. "I just—"

"I'll pay," Christy interrupted. "Luckily I brought my baby-sitting money." She opened up her small purse and took out several bills.

"Thanks." He gulped, wishing the floor would open up and swallow him whole—along with that stupid ketchup bottle.

But there was still hope. Maybe Christy could go home and change, and they could start the whole date over again. Well, minus the part that included eating.

He didn't want to give up yet. Jake had spent the last few months building up the courage to ask Christy out on a real date, and he wanted it to be perfect. But even if it couldn't be *perfect,* he still wanted it to *be.*

"Do you still want to go to the movie?" he asked. "We can catch a later show."

She looked into his eyes, then smiled. "Okay. Yes, I'd like that."

They both slid out of the booth and headed for the door. Trying to regain his gentleman status,

Jake took Christy's arm to help her down the steps that led to the parking lot.

"I think I can get out most of the—" Christy's voice suddenly broke off as she missed one of the steps.

One second she had been right next to him, her arm in his hand. The next second she was sprawled on the parking lot, holding her ankle and moaning.

"Are you okay?" he asked, kneeling beside her.

"It's these shoes," she explained, wincing. "I'm not used to heels."

He looked at the shoe she was now holding in her hand. It had one of those skinny heels that his mom wore when she and his dad went out to dinner.

"Why are you wearing those?" he asked. "You should have worn your sneakers, like you always do."

Christy's eyes filled with tears. "Excuse me!" she shouted. "I was trying to be grown-up for a change."

Uh-oh. He had made another blunder. "I didn't mean anything by it," he said quickly. "I just, uh, don't understand why you're trying to act like you're twenty years old or something."

There. That was a compliment. He had told her that he liked her just the way she was. She didn't need to do anything fancy to impress him.

Christy stood up, hopping on her good ankle. "I guess you would have preferred it if I acted like a five-year-old and spilled ketchup all over you!" she blurted out, her face a bright, angry red.

"I *said* I was sorry about that," he yelled back. "How many times do you want me to apologize?"

She sighed, looking defeated. "I didn't mean it that way," she exclaimed. "It's just that this date isn't at all like I thought it would be. . . . I thought you were going to make an effort."

Make an effort? He had shaved for the first time in his life this afternoon just to make an effort. If she didn't appreciate that, then it was her problem.

"Maybe we should skip the movie," he suggested, still hoping against hope that she would disagree with him.

She scowled. "If that's your attitude, then maybe we should."

"Fine!" he exclaimed.

"Fine!" she yelled.

He kicked an empty Coke can across the parking lot. "I'm going to walk home *that* way," he shouted, pointing in the opposite direction of the way they had come.

"Good. I'm going to walk home the *other* way." With that, she turned and limped across the parking lot.

Jake stood, watching her go. After almost a minute he had a strange sensation that he wasn't alone. He glanced toward the diner and saw the guys who had been making fun of him staring at him from the other side of the window.

Great! Not only had he ruined things with Christy, but his reputation would be damaged forever. And it was all her fault. If he never saw Christy Redmond again, it would be too soon.

One

Christy

I POURED A tablespoon of olive oil onto the center of the large frying pan, then tilted the pan from side to side until the oil was spread evenly across the Teflon surface. Next I cracked an egg on the edge of the counter and carefully spilled the contents onto the now sizzling oil. I turned up the heat and stood back to wait until the over-easy egg was ready to slide onto one of the plates I had warming in the oven.

A year ago nobody would have said that I, Christy Redmond, could boil a pot of water, much less believe that I would wake up at dawn to perfect another breakfast item I was adding to my slowly building repertoire of dishes. Then again, a year ago nobody would have said a *lot* of things about me that were now true.

For instance, nobody, and I mean nobody,

would have predicted that I would be going to my senior prom at Union High with Jake Saunders. I still couldn't believe I was stuck going to the dance with that annoying collection of irksome personality traits. *But there's a method to this madness,* I reminded myself. Or if not a method, at least a *reason*.

It was the reason that lay behind most, if not all, of the innumerable changes in my life. I held back tears as I stared at the frying egg. My mom used to be the one who got up early every morning to cook breakfast. But she hadn't been able to do that for a long time. Not since she had been diagnosed with breast cancer and undergone a double mastectomy eighteen months ago.

I eyed the egg, assessing how close it was to being done—firm white, runny yellow. *Another ninety seconds,* I guessed.

Mom had suffered through a major operation and a radical course of chemotherapy. She had won a few battles against the cancer, but I knew, deep down in the darkest part of my soul, that she probably wasn't going to win the war.

I slipped on an oven mitt, opened the oven door, and pulled out one of the plates. After I put the egg on the plate, I would add two slices of toast and half a grapefruit. This was my dad's favorite breakfast, although I had cut him down to two eggs per week after we studied the effects of cholesterol in AP biology last month.

Making breakfast every day wasn't much, but at least I felt I was doing *something* to help out my parents.

Early in the morning, with sunlight streaming in through the kitchen windows, I could almost believe that everything was okay. It wasn't until later, when I went upstairs to spend time with Mom, that I would come crashing back down to reality.

As I slid two pieces of bread into the toaster, I remembered the time in third grade when Jake and I had tried to make grilled-cheese sandwiches in the toaster. What a fiasco! It was a miracle we hadn't set the entire kitchen on fire. Of course, that was back when Jake and I had been friends—it seemed like a lifetime ago.

I had practically grown up with Jake. His mom and my mom were best friends, and their family lived down the block. We had spent our summers together—lemonade stands, kick the can, running through every sprinkler on the block. Jake had been my first confidant, and for a while I had thought I was in love with him. Then again, I had also thought I was in love with Barney the dinosaur.

A date with Barney probably would have gone better than the one Jake and I went on, I thought as I watched the toast pop up. It had been the summer after seventh grade. Jake and I had been flirting for months, which mostly involved us daring each other to eat gross foods and having splashing fights at the neighborhood pool. And then "it" had happened.

He was wearing a green-and-blue-striped shirt with short white tennis shorts (hey, guys don't develop their fashion sense until at least the tenth grade). Jake showed up at the screen door at the back of our house, stammered for approximately thirty seconds, and then asked if I would like to accompany him to the diner for dinner and then to a movie at the mall. By the time I had finished saying yes, he was already halfway down the block.

I had stood motionless at the screen door for what felt like an hour, going over and over the invitation in my mind. That afternoon I had been the happiest girl in the world.

Too bad I didn't have the wisdom to stay home and practice putting on eye shadow the night of our so-called date, I thought now, slicing through a grapefruit in one swift motion. That evening had been a total fiasco.

Jake and I never recovered after that night. We'd been forced together the very next day for a family function—*big mistake*. Our delicate thirteen-year-old egos had been too recently stomped on, by each other, no less. We'd glared at each other. Made obnoxious comments under our breath. And with each passing day, we grew further and further apart. And suddenly weeks, months, and then years had gone by.

Dad's breakfast was ready, so all there was left to do was whip up some French toast for my mom and me. Her appetite had been terrible lately, and I was hoping that one of her favorite foods would entice her into eating something substantial.

I was still thinking about Jake as I cracked three eggs, one after another, on the side of a large glass bowl. It was almost unbelievable that Jake and I were still locked in our version of a Cold War, especially because we were still thrown together all the time—an unfortunate by-product of our parents' longtime friendship. We'd always hid our animosity from our parents, but not from each other.

I stuck a fork into the bowl of eggs and began to whip them into a frothy batter. Both Jake and I had become experts at the verbal one-two punch. Lately every time Jake and I got into it, I had taken to using a three-word attack from a list of Shakespearean insults I had downloaded off the Internet. Lumpish, idle-headed measle. Churlish, bat-fowling minnow. Reeky, spur-galled ratsbane.

Too bad my mom was so set on the idea of me going to the prom with none other than the vain, toad-spotted pig-nut himself. My mother, Rose Redmond, was a completely normal person in almost every way. She was intelligent, had a great sense of humor, and doled out the kind of advice that I hoped to give to my daughter someday. But the woman had a *thing* about the senior prom.

Probably because the first real date my mom and dad ever had was the night of their own senior prom. Since then Mom had been convinced that it was a night made for magic. And somehow, someway, she thought that Jake Saunders plus Christy Redmond equaled abracadabra.

I doubted that it was Jake's idea to pop the big question. I was ninety percent sure that Mrs. Saunders had talked him into it. Nonetheless, Jake didn't *have* to agree to ask me to be his date. As much as I hated to, I had to give him credit for his part in making Mom's dream come true. I had no illusion that Jake actually *wanted* to be my date, which meant that the guy was basically sacrificing his prom.

Unfortunately, going to the prom with Jake meant that even if Matt Fowler—the Boy of Sparkling Blue Eyes and Perfect Teeth—asked me to go to the prom with *him,* I would have to say no.

I plopped a piece of wheat bread into the egg batter, my heart beating just a little faster at the thought of Matt. He had transferred to Union High last year, but he hadn't reached his full hot-guy potential until *this* year. More important, Matt hadn't started to flirt with me until exactly two weeks ago. It had been in AP bio, and he had offered me a Pez. Nothing shouts romantic interest like a small piece of rectangular-shaped, tart candy that comes out of the mouth of a miniature, plastic Batman.

As the French toast sizzled in the pan, I imagined myself slow dancing with Matt. I would stare into his blue eyes, and all of the worries and anxieties that kept me awake at night would melt away as if they had never existed. . . .

Not! I reminded myself. Instead of swaying to a ballad with Matt, I would probably be exchanging snappy one-liners with Jake next to the refreshment table. I would spend most of the evening watching Jake ogle every girl in a low-cut dress within a hundred-foot radius of whatever corner we planted ourselves in.

Maybe I'll try to get out of the date with Jake, I

decided, thinking again of Matt's spectacular gaze. *I would be doing* both *of us a favor!*

Dad walked into the kitchen just as I was turning off the heat under the French toast. He was whistling, but he looked tired.

"How is she?" I asked.

He paused next to me and dropped a kiss on the top of my head. "She's okay, honey. Not great—but okay."

"I made French toast," I said brightly. "Mom *loves* my French toast."

Dad slid into a chair at the kitchen table, and I set his breakfast down in front of him. For a moment he just stared at the plate, almost as if he didn't recognize what it was. I knew what he was thinking about. Mom.

Finally he picked up his fork. "Rose has always loved French toast," he murmured. "Maybe it will tempt her."

I picked up Mom's plate and set my face in grin position. I made sure that the first time my mother saw me every morning, I was smiling. I wanted her to believe I was happy . . . no matter what I was feeling inside.

Two

Christy

IKNOCKED SOFTLY on the door of my parents' bedroom. There was no response, so I nudged the door open with my hip and stuck my head into the room. My mother lay in the middle of her bed, propped up against a wall of pillows. Her eyes were closed, and I could tell from the expression on her face that she was sleeping lightly.

"Mom . . . ," I whispered. "Time for breakfast."

Her eyes fluttered open. For a split second I watched the muscles of my mother's face contort with pain. Then her gaze landed on me, and she smiled. I grinned back at her, holding up the breakfast tray for her inspection.

"Good morning, sweetie," she greeted me, as she did every day. "How nice of my wonderful daughter to make me such a delicious breakfast."

19

I felt a warm glow from the praise. Now that Mom was sick, I treasured these little things I could do to make her happy. "Do you feel up to eating?" I asked, my voice hopeful.

She moved to the side of the bed and took the tray from me. "For you, I would eat liver, or snails, or cow's tongue," she assured me. "At least . . . I would try."

I laughed. "As long as you manage a few bites of the French toast, I'll be satisfied."

I perched on the overstuffed chair beside my parents' bed and waited anxiously to see how much my mom would eat. She had been steadily losing weight since her surgery, and it seemed that every pound she shed was a bad omen.

"This is delicious, Christy," Mom told me, swallowing a bite. "Maybe you should take some gourmet-cooking lessons—you've got talent."

I rolled my eyes. "Mom, it's two slices of bread fried in egg batter. I don't think I'm quite ready for the Cordon Bleu in Paris."

She didn't answer. Mom was now staring at the food as if it were her worst enemy. I bit my lip, holding back the tears that suddenly threatened to slide down my cheeks. I knew what the look on her face meant. She had lost her appetite, and one more bite would probably make her want to throw up.

I took the tray. "I'll leave it over on the dresser," I told her. "You can have some more later."

She nodded. "Thanks, honey. I guess I wasn't as

hungry as I thought I was." She leaned back against the pillows, her eyes heavy with fatigue.

That was my cue. It was time to leave my mother to rest so I could finish getting ready for school. I took a deep breath, pushing away the sense of doom that I felt as I studied her face. I couldn't succumb to any dark thoughts about the future. Mom needed my optimism.

"I'll see you after school," I told her. "Just tell Mrs. Saunders that I put a lasagna in the fridge to heat up for lunch."

Mom nodded sleepily. "Molly and I will have a feast," she whispered.

I started to tiptoe from the room, believing that Mom had fallen into another light sleep.

"Christy," she called as I reached the door. "Can you do me a favor before you leave?"

I turned around. "Sure, Mom. Anything." *Maybe she wants to try the French toast again,* I hoped.

"I'd love it if you would open the window," she asked. "I want to smell the fresh spring air."

I smiled. Spring had always been my mother's favorite season. She was way into gardening, and she used to spend hours on her hands and knees in the backyard as soon as the final snow melted. Now her red gardening clogs and big straw hat were at the back of her closet. . . .

I walked over to the window and opened it wide. The air was cool and clean, and I could hear birds singing in the trees outside the house. I inhaled deeply, relishing the fact that my mother wasn't too sick to enjoy a beautiful day.

"That's wonderful," Mom murmured. "Mornings like this always make me think of romance."

Me too, I thought. I had practically been foaming at the mouth, thinking about Matt while I cooked breakfast.

"Which reminds me . . . as soon as you pick up your prom dress from Claire's Boutique, you'll have to do a fashion show for me."

"I will," I promised. "The dress is gorgeous—you'll love it."

All signs of fatigue gone, my mother's eyes shone at the thought of seeing me in my floor-length gown. As I said, she had a thing about the prom.

"You and Jake are going to have a wonderful time," she mused. "I wish I could be a fly on the wall at the dance. It means the world to me that you two are going together."

"Uh . . . yeah. It'll be a blast," I agreed.

How could I even have *considered* getting out of the date with Jake? It meant so much to my mom to see the two of us together. . . . There was no way I could let her down. No matter how distasteful I found the wagtail.

Her eyes closed again. "I think I'll just lie here and listen to the birds awhile," Mom said softly.

I walked back to the door. "Hey, Mom?" I called quietly.

"Yes, pumpkin?" she asked, her eyes still closed.

"I can't wait to show you my dress." The image of her smile in my mind, I slipped out of the room.

22

I'm going to the prom with Jake, I reaffirmed to myself. And I was going to pretend to love every minute of it—for my mother.

In my room I pulled off the sweatshirt I had worn to cook breakfast. It was splattered with oil and syrup. My cooking skills might be improving, but I still managed to make a mess every time I went near the stove.

As I slipped into a white cotton shirt, I caught sight of myself in the full-length mirror that stood in one corner of my bedroom. I stopped and stared at my face. My skin was almost as pale as the white cotton, especially in contrast to my dark brown, shoulder-length hair.

I walked closer to the mirror, feeling like I was looking at a reflection of a ghost. There was so much on my mind that I hadn't really *looked* at myself lately. And I couldn't help but notice that I wasn't exactly a pretty sight. I looked like Morticia—on a bad day.

There were faint dark circles around my hazel eyes, and there were little lines around my mouth, as if my lips were superglued into a permanent frown. Ugh! I hadn't been sleeping well lately, but I hadn't realized that my insomnia showed so much. Under normal circumstances, I was sure that my mom and dad would have been taking my temperature if I came downstairs looking this bad. But like me, they had something else to worry about.

"This is no good, Christy," I told myself. I

didn't want to walk around Union High looking like a total stress case.

I finished buttoning my shirt and walked into my bathroom, which was something of a wreck. I was mastering the art of cooking . . . but my cleaning habits left a lot to be desired. At the bottom of an old shoe box I kept next to my sink, I found a bright pink shade of blush.

A few strokes with the blush brush added much needed pink to my pale cheeks. Next I coated my eyelashes in mascara that I'd purchased circa 1997. *Note to self*, I thought. *Update your makeup supply.* Finally I coated my lips with a subtle shade of dusty rose.

I looked a lot better. But there was still something missing from my face. A smile. Lately I had only been bothering to pull out smiles for Mom and Dad. But that was going to change.

I didn't want anyone to notice the mounting fear that was keeping me up nights. It was vital that I stay strong for my parents, and part of staying strong meant that I carried on my life as if nothing were wrong. As much as I appreciated the concern my best friends, Jane and Nicole, had for me, I didn't want their pity. I didn't want *anyone's* pity. It wouldn't help Mom—and it would just make me feel worse.

I practiced several different smiles in the mirror above the sink, testing which one looked the most natural. Finally I settled on a casual grin that *almost* reached my eyes.

"Good enough," I declared. "Christy Redmond, I think you're ready for your public."

Hi, Matt. How's it going? I rehearsed in my mind, checking the status of the grin. I nodded to myself in the mirror.

My friends—and Matt—weren't going to know how scared I was. As far as the world was concerned, I was a normal, happy, healthy teenager without a care in the world.

Ha.

Three

Jake

"COME ON, RAMONA," I begged. "I know you can do it, baby." I turned the key in the ignition of my Volkswagen GTI for the third time, praying for some kind of life from the engine.

But there was no sound from the car's internal organs, and I knew getting the engine going within the next three minutes was impossible. It wasn't the first time the fifth-hand used car I had bought with the lawn-mowing money I had saved last summer had refused to cooperate with me. And I was sure it wouldn't be the last. Ramona, my car, had an extremely temperamental personality.

This was the last thing I needed. I was running way late, and Mrs. Clark had informed me last week that I was going to have to stay after school if I was tardy one more time. At the age of seventeen, staying after school was a downright humiliating experience.

I gazed down the block, trying to figure out my next course of action. My dad had already left for work, and my mom was in the shower. But if I walked to school, I was going to be at least twenty minutes late.

And then I saw none other than Christy Redmond racing out of her house. Her arms were loaded down with books, as always. I sighed. Christy was the last person I wanted to ask for a ride to school. But she was also the only person on this street about to head to Union High.

Pride or detention. Pride. Detention. Okay, I would sacrifice my pride in the name of avoiding detention. It was the only sane thing to do. I jumped out of the car and slammed the door behind me.

Swinging my backpack over one shoulder, I jogged down the block, waving my arms. When I was about fifty feet from the Redmonds' house, Christy looked up from the door she was unlocking.

"You can stop waving, Jake," she informed me. "I see you."

"Can I have a ride to school?" I asked. "Ramona is in one of her moods."

She shrugged. "Get in."

Huh. That was easy. This wasn't the first time I'd had to swallow my pride and ask Christy for a lift to school. But usually she tortured me for a couple of minutes before she grudgingly agreed to let me grace the inside of her precious car. I tossed my backpack into the backseat of her Honda and slid into the passenger seat.

Christy barely seemed to notice me as she started the car and put it into gear. Her eyes were focused on the road, and she seemed to be in some sort of meditative trance.

"You're losing your touch," I commented, glancing sideways at her dark hair and ivory skin.

She raised an eyebrow. "What's that supposed to mean?"

"I haven't received one insult since I got into this car," I pointed out. "We've been together for almost three full minutes, and you've neither commented on my poor taste in girls *nor* called me a ruttish, reeling-ripe puttock."

"Maybe I've matured," she responded. "Maybe I've realized that it's a waste of time to expend even an iota of mental energy on sparring with you."

Right. And I'm the proud owner of a brand-new Porsche, I thought. "I've got another theory," I informed her. "I think you're harboring a hidden, burning passion for me. It's written all over your face."

Now *that* got her attention. Christy took her eyes off the road just long enough to glare at me. "I might have a burning *disdain* for you," Christy retorted. "But as for giving you a ride, I'm only doing what's right. My parents always taught me to take pity on stray animals."

Ouch. I never should have opened my mouth. But now that I had . . . there was no way I was going to let Christy get the last word.

"Speaking of animals, I saw your ex-boyfriend making out with some freshman in the cafeteria the other day. He was kissing her in between showing off his ability to snort milk out of his nose to his buddies."

"He must have been making out with Leanne Nelson," Christy came back at me. "Isn't she the girl who turned you down for a date last month?"

Ouch again. Christy was an expert at getting under my skin. Why did I find it necessary to provoke her the minute I got into the car? *Because you're an idiot,* I told myself. But it was too late to take it back. So far, this day was getting off to a stellar start.

For the tenth time I regretted the fact that I had let my mom talk me into asking Christy to the prom. Not that I had resisted the idea. I knew that Rose Redmond had always had a not-so-secret hope that Christy and I would fall in love. Making her happy by taking Christy to the prom was, like, the least I could do for the woman who had been basically like a second mom to me since I was five.

It was ironic, really. I could have named at least six guys who would have killed to take Christy Redmond to the senior prom. And I, her arch-enemy, had asked her to the dance as a favor to her mother. *At what point is life going to start making sense?* I wondered as Christy slammed on the brakes to avoid going through a yellow light.

"So have you thought up a good excuse to get out of going to the prom with me yet?" Christy asked, almost as if she had been reading my mind with an X-ray machine.

"Why?" I asked. "Have you found some no-brained jock you'd rather go with?"

I had never understood Christy's taste in guys. She flitted from one amiable, good-looking bone-head to another. Apparently she enjoyed the company of guys who resembled friendly puppies. Naturally, none of these relationships (and I use that term loosely) lasted for more than three or four weeks. Sometimes I thought she chose her dates based solely on who would provide the best material for my stinging barbs.

"For your information, David Foster was a National Merit semifinalist," she retorted, referring to her last sort-of boyfriend. "Not everyone finds it necessary to flaunt their smarts in order to get attention."

I decided not to respond to that particular comment. I knew Christy thought I tended to be obnoxious—it wasn't new information. Luckily there were others who *appreciated* my strong personality. Wendy Schultz, for instance. She was an adorable junior who had been giving me The Eye in the cafeteria lately.

Now, there's an ideal prom date, I thought. Wendy was pretty, smart, and, most important, *pleasant.* I would have loved to put my arms around her for a few rounds of slow, slow dancing.

"Well, don't worry," I assured Christy. "Once we get to the dance, you can flirt with any National Merit semifinalist you want to."

"I *know*, Jake," Christy declared. "We'll do the limo, we'll do the corsage, we'll do the pictures. After we make nice for the parents, we're both free to do whatever we want once we arrive at the prom."

She had repeated back to me exactly what I had said to her when I asked her to be my "date." I guessed that bringing up the same subject again had hurt her girlish sensibility.

"Unless you *want* to be real dates," I said quickly. "I mean, it's not like I'm going to refuse to dance with you or anything."

She snorted. "I'll have plenty of people to do the lambada with," she assured me. "Don't you worry your tickle-brained little head."

"Say no more," I answered. "I'll be *more* than happy to leave you to your own devices."

"Good." It had the ring of a definitive, final statement. She was done with the conversation. Had we not been confined to the front seat of a small car, Christy probably would have waved her hand to dismiss me from the room.

That's fine with me, I thought. Who cared if Christy didn't want to talk to me? I didn't want to talk to her either. I would sit here in silence until we pulled into the school parking lot.

Still, Christy's attitude was just a tad irritating. Even beyond her usual brand of irritating. She didn't have to be quite so bummed about going to the prom with me. It wasn't as if I were a total loser. For that matter, I wasn't any kind of loser. Not that

I would ever let Christy know that she had even slightly gotten to me. I might not be too proud to cop a ride, but I had my limits.

Besides, lots of girls would have jumped at the chance to go to the prom with me, if I did say so myself. Wendy Schultz, for instance. I would have been willing to bet anyone fifty dollars—no, a hundred—that she would have done somersaults if I'd invited her to be my date.

I was getting the sinking feeling that prom night was going to be a replay of the Date from Hell after seventh grade. *At least it can't be any worse,* I thought.

Sometimes it was hard for me to believe that at one time in our lives, Christy and I had been almost inseparable. She was the first girl I really got to know. In truth, she was the first girl I ever loved.

During long summer days in grade school, I had learned that girls could be playing with a doll one minute, climbing a tree the next. I had learned that girls were a lot more sympathetic when it came to scraped knees than boys were. I had learned that . . . well, just because girls had longer hair and softer skin didn't mean they couldn't be a blast to hang out with.

I sighed quietly, glancing at Christy out of the corner of my eye. Now that we weren't engaged in verbal combat, I could really study her face. She looked as beautiful as she always did . . . but something was off.

She's got circles under her eyes, I realized. *She's tired.* Sure, she was wearing blush and lipstick and whatever else it was that girls wore to make themselves look totally put together. But beyond the makeup, I could see that Christy was exhausted.

Suddenly all of the fire seeped out of my bones. Next to me sat the girl I had grown up with. And she was going through the worst time of her entire life. I felt a deep pang of sympathy—but I knew better than to say anything aloud to Christy.

She wasn't the type of person who wanted to acknowledge any kind of weakness. If I let her know that I sensed her pain, it would only make her feel worse. There was, however, something I *could* do.

I could offer Christy what I always offered her. A person with whom she could argue and vent and relieve some of the tension that must be building up inside her. Hey, it wasn't much . . . but it was all I had to give.

Four

Christy

"**D**O YOU THINK Max would still like me if I cut off all of my hair?" Jane wondered aloud.

It was Tuesday, and Jane, Nicole, and I were having lunch at our usual table in the Union High lunchroom. Since the cafeteria was serving an orange glop they had the audacity to label "macaroni 'n' cheese," I was glad that I'd had the wisdom to bring a smoked-turkey sandwich on seven-grain bread from home.

"You mean, like, cut it *all* off, Sinead O'Connor style?" Nicole asked. "Or do you mean cut it off Winona Ryder style?"

"Duh," Jane responded. "I'm not going to go *bald*."

"I'm not going to the prom," Nicole said, changing the subject completely. "I'm simply not going to go. No biggie."

"Part of me thinks Max would find the new haircut sexy," Jane said, ignoring Nicole's comment. "Aren't guys supposed to be intrigued by unexpected change?"

I almost laughed. Jane Smith and Nicole Gilmore had been my two best friends for as long as I could remember—well, since ninth grade anyway. The three of us had developed our own form of communication during the last four years. Often our conversations consisted of three simultaneous monologues. But somehow everybody managed to hear what everyone else was saying.

"Let's face it," Nicole declared. "The guys in this school are *lame*." She glanced at Jane. "I mean, except for Max."

Jane and Max Ziff had starting going out a couple of days ago, and the relationship had made Jane deliriously happy. It also seemed to be making her overly preoccupied with her hairstyle.

"Maybe I'll just get a new sweater," Jane decided. "If I get my hair cut, then Max won't be able to run his fingers through it. And he loves doing that . . ."

As Jane went on in her dreamy tone and Nicole cut in every now and then to zap Jane back down to earth, I resisted the urge just to close my eyes, put my head down on the table, and let their conversation swirl around me like a gentle stream. I had never thought the sound of my friends' voices could be so . . . soothing.

Sure, their problems were minor compared to

what I was dealing with. But that's exactly what I liked about having them around. Nicole and Jane had made a tacit agreement not to push me to talk about my mom's illness. They knew I wasn't the type to pour out my problems, and they respected my wish to maintain my privacy. At the same time, I knew they were there for me if I ever wanted to talk.

"What do you think, Christy?" Jane asked, interrupting my thoughts. "Should I get my hair cut—or buy a new sweater with one of those plunging necklines?"

This time I *did* laugh. Jane sounded so serious—as if she were discussing a Middle East peace agreement rather than what kind of fashion statement she wanted to make on her date Friday night.

I pushed away the image of my mother's face, etched in pain. There was nothing I could do for her right now—except preserve my sanity by throwing myself into the Life of a Normal Teenager.

"Go with the sweater," I advised her. "Max likes your hair just the way it is."

"I agree," Nicole added. "Max loves you for your sparkling personality—but he also loves you for your cute ponytail."

Jane's eyes lit up. "Do you really think he *loves* me?" she asked. "Or is it a strong case of *like?*"

I settled more comfortably in my chair, ready to launch into a long and detailed discussion about the exact state of Max and Jane's relationship. Friends. What would I do without them?

★   ★   ★

I stood several feet away from one of the industrial-sized garbage cans at the back of the cafeteria. I took aim and tossed my diet Coke can toward the huge receptacle.

"She shoots . . . she scores," I announced as the can landed in the trash can.

"You should think about going pro," I heard a voice behind me comment as I held up my arms in victory.

I didn't need to turn around to know who had spoken to me. I had kept one eye out for Matt Fowler all through lunch period, but the cafeteria had been so crowded that I hadn't been able to catch sight of him.

"Hi, Matt," I said, pivoting in what I hoped was a somewhat alluring manner.

He grinned. "Christy, you're just the person I was looking for."

Okay, time to go into full-flirt mode, I told myself. This was exactly the kind of intro I had been waiting for during the last two weeks.

"Is there something I can do for you?" I asked, executing a subtle eyelash flutter as I attempted to dazzle him with a hundred–watt smile.

"I come to you as the bearer of excellent news," Matt informed me. "AP biology is canceled this afternoon."

Okay. It wasn't the pickup line I had been hoping for . . . but it *was* good news. Biology was my last class of the day. If it was canceled, that meant I could leave school early and spend a little extra time with my mom. She was usually in pretty good shape during the afternoon.

"What happened?" I asked. "Was there a bomb scare in the lab?"

Matt laughed. "Nothing quite so dramatic. Word has it that Mr. Burgess has a nasty case of the flu. The kind that makes you throw up every five minutes."

I knew altogether too much about throwing up. I had held Mom's hair back for her at least a dozen times as she had thrown up after chemotherapy treatments. And later . . . she hadn't had any hair to hold back. The powerful chemicals in the chemotherapy had caused almost all of it to fall out.

"Thanks for letting me know," I told Matt. "That was sweet of you."

I expected him to turn around and walk off, but he didn't. Instead Max fixed his startling blue eyes on mine and stayed rooted to his spot.

"Is there something else?" I asked. *Maybe my makeup is wearing off,* I thought. *Maybe he's wondering why I look so darn tired.*

"I thought you and I could take advantage of the free time," he said, giving me a delicious smile. "I, uh, was wondering if you'd like to join me for a little afternoon air hockey at Jon's Pizza."

"Oh!" This was the invitation I had been waiting for. But now that it had been issued, I wasn't sure how to respond.

I was torn between the prospect of a date with my crush and a little extra quality time with my mother. Ninety percent of me wanted to go home and see how Mom was doing. But the other ten percent of me found myself staring into Matt's twinkling, mesmerizing blue eyes.

"Air hockey sounds great," I heard myself saying. Maybe a little recreation with a cute boy was exactly what I needed to decompress.

As Matt walked away, I gave myself a mental pat on the back. Sure, Jake Saunders thought I was about as attractive as the bride of Frankenstein. But what did he know? Matt Fowler had just asked me to accompany him on something that definitely resembled a date. I still had it.

"Keep your eye on the puck," Matt instructed. "Don't get distracted."

We were at the back of Jon's Pizza, where there were a couple of air-hockey games, three pinball machines, and a somewhat rickety Foosball table. The minute Matt had dropped two quarters into the slot and the table had come to life, I knew I was in trouble.

Matt had scored five goals off me in less than ten minutes—I had only managed to block the puck one time. Luckily he wasn't one of those guys who found it necessary to lord his hand-eye coordination over others. He had stopped the game and given me some key pointers. I was still losing, but at least I wasn't totally humiliating myself.

"Here it comes!" Matt warned. "Remember, *keep your eye on the puck.*"

40

I zeroed in on the small, round, plastic disk and leaned over the table. I felt the faint breeze of the air coming off the game as I kept my eyes glued to the puck that was whizzing toward me. *Three, two, one.* I moved my "stick" a fraction of an inch and made contact with the puck. *Zoom!*

The plastic disk shot across the table—and into Matt's goal. "Score!" I shouted, throwing up my arms. "I did it!"

Matt grinned. "Move over, Wayne Gretzky— here comes Christy."

"Did you let me score on purpose?" I asked suspiciously.

"No way," Matt insisted. "I'm too competitive to let someone get a goal off me—even someone as pretty as you are."

My heart skipped a beat. Matt had said I was pretty. This was exactly what I had been waiting for, and it felt good. It had been a long time since I had enjoyed such a typical, seventeen-year-old moment.

"Let's celebrate your triumph with a couple of slices," Matt suggested. "I don't want you to get air-hockey elbow."

I slid into a corner booth and watched Matt as he went to the counter for our slices of pizza. I felt more relaxed than I had in days. With Matt I could almost—but not quite—forget about what was going on at home. At least for this hour I was just a normal girl with normal, everyday problems.

Matt is so easy to be with, I thought. He was the exact opposite of Jake, whose idea of a good time was needling me to the point of extreme exasperation. Matt just liked to have a good time—he wasn't obsessed with outsmarting me every second of our conversation. *This is what I needed,* I decided, glad I had taken Matt up on his offer.

When Matt appeared at the booth with a slice of pepperoni pizza for me, I flashed him my best smile. "Thanks for inviting me out today," I told him as I sprinkled my pizza with Parmesan cheese.

He finished chewing the huge bite he had taken from his slice of Italian sausage. He swallowed, then dabbed at his lips with a paper napkin. *Hmmm . . . a gentleman,* I noted. *A bonus point for good table manners.*

"You don't need to thank me," he responded finally. "I've been wanting to ask you out for weeks."

I felt a tingle of pleasure that is particular to a guy letting a girl know he's interested. It was excitement mixed with satisfaction. And hope for the future.

"I'm glad you did," I told him. "This has been the best afternoon I've had in a long time."

He smiled. "Good. Me too."

There was a moment of awkward silence. We had both established that we were happy to be here. Now what?

"Well, air hockey was the perfect antidote to all the pressure I've been under," I offered. "My mom is really sick . . . and sometimes I need to let off some serious steam."

"Yeah, I—I, uh, heard about that," Matt stammered. "I'm, uh, sorry."

"Thanks." I took another bite of pizza and prepared to let the subject drop.

I could tell that Matt was uncomfortable with the idea of my mother having cancer. But that was normal. A lot people had trouble confronting the *c* word.

Matt pushed away the paper plate that had held his pizza. "Hey, how about another game?" he asked. "I don't have to be at baseball practice for almost an hour."

To be honest, I'd had my fair share of air hockey for the day. I would have preferred a pinball challenge. But I didn't want to hurt Matt's feelings. Especially since he had been so nice about giving me pointers.

"That sounds great," I responded. "I can't wait to try out my new moves now that I've been reenergized."

As we headed back to the table, I noticed that Matt looked almost as good from behind as he did from the front. *This is a guy who can take my mind off my troubles,* I confirmed to myself.

Sort of.

No. Definitely.

Because that was what I needed. To escape a little. Stop worrying. Not talk about the big "it."

Right?

Five

Christy

"THERE'S NOTHING BETTER than a teacher with the flu," Matt commented as he drove me back to school. "I feel like we had a snow day."

"Don't tell me you were actually *glad* to miss out on the opportunity to do an advanced dissection of an earthworm," I joked. "I've been looking forward to it all month."

"Maybe we'll get lucky, and he'll be out all week," he said. "We could start a tournament of champions at Jon's Pizza."

Amazingly, I had actually managed to win one of our air-hockey games. Matt had looked so surprised that I'd half expected him to faint from shock.

"Ha!" I laughed. "I don't think beating you one game out of, like, six calls for an entire tournament." I paused. "But I might take you on in pinball."

"It's a date." As Matt spoke, I noticed a few droplets of water spattering against the windshield.

Moments later, rain began to fall steadily. Rivulets of water streamed down the glass, and Matt turned on the windshield wipers. I had always loved the soothing, rhythmic sound of wipers.

"I love rain," I told Matt, cracking the window of the passenger-side door. "Especially warm spring rain."

Matt shook his head. "I can't stand it. This means we're going to do sprints in the gym during baseball practice."

"Ugh." I didn't blame Matt for being bummed out about the rain, but I couldn't get enough of the fresh, damp air.

I inhaled deeply, then rolled the window down farther so that I could stick my head out of the car. I held out my tongue and caught several drops on my tongue. Delicious!

Matt laughed. "You're crazy, you know that?" he asked as we pulled into the school parking lot. "Most girls would pay money just to keep from getting their hair wet."

I grinned at him. "Last time I checked, I wasn't 'most girls.'"

Matt drove through the parking lot and stopped next to my Honda. "You're going to get soaked just getting into your car," he noted.

"Don't worry about it." I put my hand on the door latch and turned to him. "Thanks for a great afternoon, Matt."

"It was my pleasure." He hesitated, and it seemed like he wanted to say something else.

"What?" I asked. "Do I have pizza sauce on my face or something?"

"No . . . I, uh, wanted to tell you something." He seemed nervous, so I took my hand off the latch and gave him my most comforting smile.

"What is it?" I asked. *Is he going to invite me to the prom?* I wondered. *And if he does . . . well, if he does, I'll have to say no. Period.*

"I, uh, already have a date to the prom," he blurted out finally. "But if I didn't, I would ask you to go with me."

I tried not to feel the sting of rejection. After all, he wasn't the only one who already had a date. I was shackled to Jake, whether I liked it or not.

"Oh." I couldn't help it. I was hurt.

"You see, Sandra Donell asked me if I would take her to the prom, like, last month," he explained. "I couldn't say no. I mean, I knew she had a crush on me . . . and it probably took a lot of guts for her to get up the nerve to ask. . . ."

"I understand," I said quickly. "I already have a date too." But I wasn't about to go into the details of my bizarre agreement with Jake. "It's a similar circumstance."

He nodded. "Well, then."

"So . . . I guess we're not going to the prom together," I said, stating the obvious.

He nodded again. "True. But that doesn't mean we can't hang out together. I mean, if you want to."

"Yes!" I realized I sounded slightly desperate, so I decided I needed to take it down a notch. "That might be nice."

"There's no law against two people having a good time together," Matt continued. "A date to the prom isn't a binding contract or anything."

"Right," I responded. Of course, in *my* case the date with Jake *felt* like a contract.

"Promise to save me a slow dance at the prom?" Matt asked softly, resting his hand on my arm.

"Definitely," I answered. "I'll save one for you, and you can save one for me." I leaned forward and gave Matt a quick peck on the cheek.

Then I slid out of the car and into the rain. As I felt the water coming down on my head, soaking me from head to foot, I imagined the rain was washing away all of my fear and anxiety. *I'm cleansed,* I thought, holding out my hands to catch more of the rain.

As I covered the several yards to get to my car, I realized something astonishing. I felt almost human again. . . . Now, *that* was an accomplishment.

The moment I put my car into reverse in order to pull out of my parking space and head home, the feeling of well-being I had enjoyed during the last hour and a half started to evaporate. Jon's Pizza, the rain, Matt's blue eyes . . . all of that seemed like a surreal daydream. Now I just wanted to get home and see how Mom was feeling.

I shook my head, willing away the fear I always

48

felt when it was time to go home. *Will she be worse? Will she be in pain? Is she having a good day? A bad day?* The same questions ran through my mind again and again every day.

I backed out of my parking space and drove slowly through the nearly empty lot. The rain had turned the sky dark, and it felt more like seven o'clock than four. *I need a nap,* I decided. Maybe when I got home, I would crawl into bed with Mom and doze for an hour or so before Dad got home. Even now, there was no place I felt safer than at my mother's side.

She always had the power to soothe whatever chaos was going on inside my head—even when it was her own illness that was the source of that chaos. *A mother's instinct,* I thought. She always knew just what to say.

As I started down the street that led to my block, I caught sight of a lone, dark figure on the side of the street. *I know that walk,* I thought. Because of the rain I couldn't see his face. But there was no doubt in my mind that it was Jake.

I should let him slosh through puddles all the way to Sunset Drive, I thought. After the way he was going after me this morning, the guy deserved to catch pneumonia on his way home.

That was what I *believed,* but I already knew that I was going to pull over and take the boy out of his misery. I couldn't help myself. Jake just looked so . . . pathetic. I stopped next to the curb and blared the horn.

Through the rain I saw Jake's head swivel toward my car. A second later he was jogging in my direction, the ever present backpack banging against his hip. He looked all of about eight years old.

I rolled down my window and thrust my head into the rain. "All aboard for Noah's ark," I called.

He sprinted around the car, yanked open the passenger-side door, and dove into the seat. "Thanks, Christy!" He slammed the door shut and heaved what sounded like a huge sigh of relief. "I was seriously worried that the five pages of notes I have to study for my history test were going to get so wet that the erasable ink was going to run all over the place."

"No problem," I answered. "I mean, it's not like I have to go out of my way to take you home."

And if I were perfectly honest with myself, I would have to admit that I preferred even the company of Jake to the onslaught of concerns that had been ricocheting around my brain. Of course, admitting that to *myself* didn't mean I was going to confess it to *him*.

Jake shook out his shaggy head of dark hair, sending about a million droplets of water in my general direction. I opened my mouth to tell him that it was supposed to be raining *outside*. Then I stopped myself, snapping my jaw shut. He'd sounded so genuinely grateful for the ride home that I decided to allow just this one obnoxious gesture to slide. There were, after all, those moments when I almost liked Jake. They were few and far between, but they did exist.

"You know who you look like right now?" Jake asked, settling into his seat.

"Who?" I steered the Honda back into my lane and headed down the street.

"Ms. Whiskers."

I raised an eyebrow. "And who is Ms. Whiskers?" I asked, knowing that I was going to regret the question.

He grinned. "She was one of my favorite stuffed animals. Ms. Whiskers was a big, pink rat . . . until I left her out in the rain one afternoon. Then she was a big, pink, *drowned* rat."

"Gee . . . thanks." I had stopped to give Jake a ride out of the goodness of my heart, and his reaction had been to compare me to a drowned rat. Touching. So much for that fleeting moment of near tolerance.

"It's not too late for me to stop this car and make you walk," I pointed out. "We rats aren't known for our generous spirits."

"Hey, watch what you say about Ms. Whiskers," Jake countered. "She was a loyal friend—until that fateful day."

"Are you this annoying all the time?" I asked. "Or do you save the 'special' parts of your personality for me and me alone?"

Jake scoffed. "You think *I'm* annoying?" he demanded. "Correct me if I'm wrong, but I could

51

have sworn I saw you driving into the parking lot with Matt Fowler."

Okay. Now he was asking for it. "What's wrong with Matt?" I demanded.

"Nothing . . . he's a nice enough guy if you like the type."

I am not going to respond, I told myself. *This is a trap.* I stared straight ahead, focusing on the movement of the windshield wipers.

Jake cleared his throat. "So, is that the guy you're so psyched to hang out with at the prom?" he asked. "Pretty-boy Matt Fowler?"

I rolled my eyes. "I don't see how that's any of your business," I retorted. "Last time I checked, I didn't need to clear my dance partners with *you.*" I paused. "Having said that, yes, Matt and I will probably keep company with each other at the prom."

Jake snorted. "Matt's a really deep guy," he remarked, his voice laced with sarcasm. "But I guess his supposed good looks make up for his lack of personality."

"Ha!" I spat out. "It's not like Wendy Schultz is known for her sparkling conversation."

Jake frowned. "How do you know about Wendy?"

"Please!" I snorted. "You're not exactly a master of subtlety, Saunders. I happened to see you practicing your lame brand of flirting with the girl in the cafeteria the other day."

"So?" he asked.

"*So,* it doesn't take a NASA engineer to figure out that you've got the hots for her." I paused. "Although *why* you'd want to go out with my-name-is-Wendy-and-I-end-every-statement-with-a-giggle is a complete mystery to me."

"Wendy is a very nice person," Matt stated, as if he were giving her a good reference for a potential future employer. "And she's *exceedingly* easy to be around."

"Suit yourself," I told him. "You can date Wendy or Bambi or Candy for all I care."

"Thanks for the stamp of approval," Jake retorted. "Now I'll be able to sleep at night."

The rain had let up considerably in the last few minutes, leaving only a gray drizzle that seemed considerably less romantic than the torrents that had been coming down when Matt and I had been sitting in his car. I found myself wishing for something more dramatic—thunder, lightning, hail. The drizzle was just plain . . . dreary.

I hit the blinker and took a right onto Sunset Drive. Finally. Two car rides with Jake in one day were two too many. The two of us simply weren't meant to be in a confined space together for any amount of time.

I stopped the car in front of my house. "Do you have the strength to make it from here?" I asked.

Jake glanced up the block toward his house. "I think I'll manage," he assured me. Then his eyes moved toward the driveway beside our house. "But I guess my mom can't even walk a block. Her car is here."

I followed Jake's gaze. He was right. Molly Saunders's supermom minivan was parked in our driveway. She had probably driven over a fresh load of frozen casseroles. Ever since Mom had gotten sick, Mrs. Saunders had made it her personal mission to ensure that we never went hungry. I knew Molly used cooking for my mother as a way to deal with the cancer, so I refrained from mentioning that we had enough frozen dinners to carry us through to the *next* millennium.

"Your mom is the greatest," I told Jake. "I don't know what we would do without her."

Jake nodded. "She . . . well, she wants to do whatever she can to help. You know how much your mom means to her."

I did. They had been friends since high school and had gone through every significant event of their lives together. I couldn't imagine how I would feel twenty years from now if Nicole or Jane were diagnosed with breast cancer. It would be devastating . . . almost as devastating as the diagnosis of my own mother.

"How is she?" Jake asked. "I mean, my mom talks about her . . . but she doesn't like to focus on her illness."

Now, *that* was the sixty-four-thousand-dollar question. How was Mom doing? I wanted to say she was doing fine. I wanted to say she was getting stronger every day. I wanted to give him a million different positive responses.

But none of them would have been true. Mom

was getting weaker every day, and there was absolutely nothing that I, or anyone else, could do about it.

I didn't even realize that tears had started to roll down my face. It wasn't until I felt Jake's hand on my shoulder that I realized my cheeks were wet. I wanted to stop the tears, but the unexpected gentleness of Jake's touch triggered something inside me.

Maybe it was the knowledge that if someone like *Jake* felt sorry for me, then the situation had to be truly awful. Maybe it was the fact that I had been bottling up my fears for days, weeks, months, and I couldn't hold back for one more second. Or maybe it was simply that it had been a while since someone had come right out and asked me that simple question. *How is she?*

I couldn't help myself. I began to sob. This wasn't quiet weeping. My shoulders were heaving, my eyes were starting to swell, and I was hiccuping. But as I cried, I felt the tension slowly starting to dissolve.

"Christy, I'm so sorry," Jake said softly. "I didn't mean to—"

"It's not your fault," I interrupted. "I'm just . . . I don't know."

Talk about humiliating! Of all times to crack, I had to do it with none other than Jake Saunders sitting next to me. I breathed deeply, willing the tears to stop.

"I don't usually cry," I said finally. "I don't want anyone's pity. It's just that sometimes . . ."

"Hey, don't think twice about it," Jake said, his hand still on my shoulder. "Crying is the most natural thing in the world."

I rolled my eyes. "Yeah, right. I'm sure you bawl all the time." Jake's kindness was threatening to bring on a whole fresh round of tears.

Be strong, I told myself. *Don't let him see how much you're hurting.* Well, it was a little late for that. Jake had already witnessed my total breakdown.

"I do cry," Jake insisted. "Just last week I had this terrible hangnail. Oh, man, I was crying like a baby."

"Uh-huh . . ." I almost smiled. The image of Jake tearing up over a tiny hangnail was beyond absurd.

"And the other day I was watching one of those cheesy long-distance commercials," he continued. "Before I knew what hit me, tears were rolling down my face and I was picking up the phone to call my grandma in Arizona."

I giggled. "Let me guess—you carry around a hankie just in case you happen to stub your toe."

"As a matter of fact, I make it a policy never to leave home without a travel pack of Kleenex." Jake unzipped his backpack as he spoke. A moment later he pulled out, yes, a brand-new packet of Kleenex. "Ta-da!" He handed me a few tissues.

"Thanks." I dabbed at my eyes, then blew my nose loudly and unceremoniously into the Kleenex.

"Those really come in handy when the bullies at school try to steal my lunch money," Jake told me, his voice gravely serious. "One time I wept all through my mystery-turkey casserole."

I giggled again. And then I started to laugh. *Really* laugh. "I hope you never get into carpentry," I sputtered. "I would hate to see what would happen if you accidentally hit your thumb with a hammer!"

"Forget about it!" Jake responded. "We're talking a major flood—a national disaster."

I kept laughing. It wasn't that Jake was so funny—although even I had to admit that the guy had a sense of humor. It just felt *so* good to really and truly laugh that I never wanted to stop.

After what felt like an hour, but was probably about two minutes, the laughter slowly started to subside. Which immediately caused another round of the hiccups.

"I'm a mess." I moaned. "First I'm sobbing, then I'm laughing hysterically." I paused. "I really didn't want anyone to see me like this."

Jake shrugged. "Hey, as far as I'm concerned, this never happened."

I nodded. "Do you mind just leaving me alone?" I asked. "I don't want to go inside until I'm one hundred percent calm."

"Say no more." Jake gave me a last glance, then slipped out of the car. "Thanks for the ride, Christy," he said, sticking his head back inside. Then he shut the door gently behind him and began to jog toward his house.

I closed my eyes and leaned my head against the back of the seat. I still couldn't believe I had totally lost it in front of Jake. I had sworn to myself I would never do that kind of thing. Then again . . . I had to admit that Jake had been incredibly cool.

For a few minutes I had felt like we were back in sixth grade, laughing and talking like we could with no one else in the world. *I* needed *that,* I realized suddenly. Because . . . wonder of wonders . . . the dull, throbbing headache that had become an intrinsic part of my life had magically disappeared.

Thanks, Jake, I thought. *This one time you really helped me out.* I unbuckled my seat belt and opened the door of the car. I couldn't wait to get inside—I wanted to see my mom. Who knew? Maybe I would even share a few laughs with the woman I loved more than anything in the whole world.

Six

Jake

"I NEED CHOCOLATE-CHIP cookies," I murmured to myself, heading up the stairs from my basement-turned-bedroom two at a time. "Or maybe a ham sandwich."

I had been trying to study for my history test for hours. So far, I had learned two dates and the names of five vice presidents. In other words, my study session was a complete bust—useless. And I knew why. Every time I bent my head over my history notes, I saw Christy's tearstained face staring back at me. Now it was almost midnight, and I was getting desperate. *When the going gets tough, the tough go to the fridge,* I told myself.

"Jake, is that you?" I heard my mother call softly.

I stopped in the arched doorway at the edge of

the living room. "What are you doing up, Mom?" I asked. "You're usually asleep before the ten o'clock news."

She was sitting on the sofa, a huge pile of photographs covering her lap. "I was looking at some old pictures."

I walked into the room and flopped beside her on the couch. "Cooing over my old baby photos?" I asked.

She smiled, but I noticed that her eyes were slightly damp. Jeez. Everywhere I went today, I was making women cry. "Most of these are of Rose and me," she explained. "We must have taken a thousand pictures together over the years."

"You two are really close, huh?" I asked. It was sort of weird to think of my mom in the context of being someone's friend. To me, she was one hundred percent Mom.

She nodded, staring at a photo of herself and Rose dressed up as Laverne and Shirley one Halloween night. "Rose is my best friend. . . . I don't know what I'm going to do without her."

"Without her?" I squeaked. "You mean . . . ?"

I had known that Rose was *really* sick. I had even known there was a chance that . . . well, she wouldn't make it. But until this moment I had never heard my mother speak as if she didn't expect Mrs. Redmond to make a full recovery. Mom had maintained a determined, positive attitude since the day her friend was diagnosed with breast cancer.

A lone tear slid down my mother's cheek as she

continued to gaze at the old photograph. "I'm praying for a miracle, sweetie. And you never know . . ."

"I didn't realize that things had gotten so bad," I said, thinking again of Christy's tears. "Christy is so strong. . . . She never talks about it."

Mom sighed. Then she shuffled through the pile and pulled out a picture of Rose holding Christy when she was a newborn baby. "Christy has always been that way. Even when she was a baby, she rarely cried. It was almost as if she didn't want to cause anyone a bit of trouble."

"Well, she hasn't changed." I thought of the firm set of Christy's jaw and her horror when she realized that I was a witness to her tears.

"If only the same were true of Rose," Mom murmured, glancing down at another picture. "She's changing every day . . . growing weaker and weaker."

"I'm so sorry, Mom," I whispered. "I wish there were something I could do to help."

My mother reached out and put her arm around my shoulders. "You *are* doing something, honey. You're taking Christy to the prom, which as you know thrills Rose. She's so happy about that."

"Mrs. Redmond might be thrilled, but Christy isn't," I commented. "She hates me."

Mom pulled me close and gave me one of her patented maternal squeezes. "Oh, honey, that's not true. You're one of Christy's oldest friends."

I shook my head. "You don't understand. She can't stand the sight of me." I paused. "Today I made her cry. . . . I mean, not on purpose, but still . . ."

My mother set aside the photographs and shifted in her seat so she could look me in the eyes. "Christy is going through a lot, Jake. I think crying is probably a really good thing for her. It's not healthy for her to hold all of her feelings in."

"Maybe . . ." Christy *had* started to laugh after the tears had stopped flowing. And she hadn't seemed angry about me asking her about her mom. She'd just been—sad.

"Christy needs all the friends she can get right now," Mom declared, her tone allowing no room for argument. "Trust me on this one, Jake—even if I am just your mom."

I nodded. I would do whatever I could for Christy. But I doubted I could do much good. As far as Christy Redmond was concerned, I was persona non grata. She had made that clear time and time again. And I didn't think my best foe's opinion on the score was going to change anytime soon. At least, not if today were any indication . . .

The Olympic-sized swimming pool was lit only by the blue glow of an underwater light. But the moon was so bright that I could see clearly the back of the girl who was treading water in the deep end. Her red bikini highlighted her ivory skin, and her dark hair was wet and glistening under the moonbeams.

I walked toward the pool, unsure why I was here or what I was meant to do. I didn't even know why I was wearing my swimming trunks. But the pool—or more accurately, the girl in the pool—was drawing me forward. The air was warm and sultry, and a light breeze blew through my hair as I continued to put one foot in front of the other.

Turn around, *I thought, staring at the back of the girl's head. But she didn't. She simply continued to tread water, seemingly unaware of my presence.*

I was acutely aware of my surroundings as I finally reached the edge of the pool. The scent of honeysuckle and jasmine filled my nostrils, and the grass under my bare feet was crisp and cool. Every nerve in my body felt hypersensitive, as if my entire life had led up to this one moonlit moment.

Standing on my tiptoes, I held my arms over my head. Then I dove into the water, swimming for several seconds until I burst through to the surface. I found myself just feet from the girl.

"Who are you?" I asked.

When she turned around, it was like the sun coming up. "Who am I?" she echoed. "Jake, you know me."

And I did. It was Christy. Beautiful, sexy Christy—my very own mermaid. "I've missed you."

She smiled. "How could you miss me?" she asked. "I've been here all the time."

"Yes, but . . . not like this." I couldn't take my eyes off her.

Was this the same girl I had climbed trees and played kick the can with? She was all grown up now.

Christy tossed her head backward, showering me with drops of cool water. Her light, sparkling laughter filled the night as she swam toward me. "You're different too, Jake. . . . I like it."

It was as if her eyes were laser beams and she was staring straight into my heart and mind. Almost of their own volition, my arms reached out, and I clasped Christy around the waist. I pulled her toward me, her body weightless in the pool's deep, blue water.

"What took you so long?" she asked, settling her slender arms around my neck. "I've only been waiting for, like, a lifetime."

I didn't respond. . . . I couldn't speak. I could only gaze into her tranquil hazel eyes and thank whatever force of nature had brought me to this spot. Then I closed my eyes and tilted my head toward her.

A moment later we were kissing. Really kissing. Her lips were soft and warm and full and just . . . incredible. The kiss went on and on until I wasn't sure where her mouth left off and mine began. I only knew that I wanted this feeling to last forever—

I woke up suddenly, gasping for breath. Bright, glaring sunlight streamed in through the small window of my basement room, and the clock beside my bed read 6:30 A.M.

"What the . . . ?" My sheets were tangled into knots, and my forehead was covered with sweat.

I kicked away the sheets and sat up, bunching my pillow behind me for support. My mind was filled with a dozen confusing images. A pool. The moon. A girl. Kissing. They were all jumbled together like a mental jigsaw puzzle.

"Wait. Not just a girl . . . ," I whispered to my-self. *"Christy."*

I had been dreaming about Christy. We had been in a pool together, and we had been making out like crazy. I shook my head, pushing away the intense memory of the dream.

This was nuts. Why would I dream about Christy, of all people? Especially . . . like *that*. I didn't even like her, much less want to kiss her. But there was no doubt about it. My heart was still pounding, and I could almost taste her lips on mine, the sensation had been so powerful.

I jumped out of bed and began to pace back and forth across my spacious bedroom. There had to be an explanation . . . and there was. In fact, the dream made perfect sense now that I really started to put the pieces together.

The dream didn't mean anything. When I had finally fallen asleep a little after 1 A.M., Christy had been alive and well in my subconscious. And why not? I had spent almost half an hour talking about her with my mother. It was only natural that she should show in my dreams.

As for the *other* elements of the dream . . . how could I explain the kissing? I stopped pacing and plopped back onto my bed. Okay, Christy *had* looked really pretty yesterday afternoon. Raindrops had clung to her eyelashes, and her cheeks had been incredibly pink—almost like a doll's.

"So I dreamed that I kissed an attractive girl," I

said to the Michael Jordan poster that hung over my bureau. "Big deal."

Dreams didn't mean a thing. Everybody knew that. Still, I was glad I had managed to get my car going last night. I didn't want to run into Christy today. I didn't want to see her until that dream had had plenty of time to fade. . . .

Seven

Christy

"**W**HAT ARE YOU doing here?" I asked Matt the next afternoon when I walked into AP bio and found him standing at my lab table, holding a stack of slides. "You're not Aisha."

He grinned. "Let me introduce myself. I'm your new lab partner, Matt Fowler."

I shook his hand, then scanned the room. Yep. There was Aisha, standing beside Matt's now former lab partner, Trent O'Grady. "I'm confused."

"It's simple," he explained. "I got here early and begged Aisha to trade partners with me. She, being a sympathetic romantic, agreed."

"Great!" I loved Aisha, but there was no doubt that biology would be a lot more . . . stimulating . . . with Matt as a lab partner. Plus he was making it very clear that he liked me.

67

At the front of the large classroom Mr. Burgess—still looking slightly green—cleared his throat. "I'm sure you all missed me yesterday," he announced. "But the good news is that I'm back. And we can all get started on our earthworms."

"So how was the rest of your afternoon yesterday?" Matt asked as we started to diagram the earthworm on sheets of grid paper.

"It was . . . weird." I stared at the piece of paper, thinking of the scene between Jake and me in my car.

"Weird?" Matt glanced up from the diagram. "That sounds interesting. Were you, like, visited by aliens or something?"

"Not quite." I wasn't ready to tell Matt about my crying fit. Somehow I knew he wouldn't understand.

Matt shrugged—a sort of far-be-it-from-me-to-interpret-a-girl's-bizarre-statement shrug. "So, what should we name the little guy?" he asked.

I stared down at the worm. "He looks like a George," I announced.

"Huh. I was thinking he looked more like a Skipper," Matt mused. "But I guess I can live with George."

As we began to slice and dice poor George, I thought of the significance of what we were doing. Sure, it seemed pretty silly right now. It was last period, the sun was shining outside, and we were all thinking ahead to our graduation in a few weeks. Who cared about the insides of an earthworm? But maybe just one of us would really *get* something out of the project. Maybe one of us would even be inspired to go to medical school.

"Wouldn't it be amazing if someone in this class discovered the ultimate cure for cancer one day?" I asked Matt.

He kept his eyes trained on what I assumed was the head of the earthworm. "Um . . . yeah. That would be great."

I was really getting into the idea. "I mean, to us this is just a class we have to pass before we can graduate from high school. But all great scientists have to start somewhere. Who knows what could happen in the future?"

"Um . . . I think I accidentally cut off George's legs—or where his legs would be if he weren't a worm." Matt took a step away from the lab table and handed me the knife we were using. "Maybe you should take over."

I bent over the earthworm, looking at him in a whole new way. He was a portal, a first step, a sign of hope in a universe that sometimes seemed absolutely hopeless. Of course, in my *own* small world it didn't really *matter* if one of us looked at our earthworm and saw the future of cancer research sitting in a small, metal tray. Not for my mom. It was too late.

"I was wondering if you wanted to go out with me on Saturday night," Matt said, breaking into my thoughts. "I thought we could do the dinner-and-a-movie thing."

Truthfully, I was more in the mood to sit

around and brood about the current failings of modern medicine than I was to watch Bruce Willis blow up some building just in time to save the chick from the bad guy.

But it was important that I keep up at least a facsimile of a social life. If nothing else, my breakdown yesterday had made me realize that I needed to find more ways to relieve my anxiety. And Matt was fun—even if he wasn't, as Jake had claimed, "deep."

"Sure," I told him. "I'd like that."

"Cool," he enthused, giving me one of his dazzling smiles. Then he pushed away the tray that held George's somewhat tattered remains. "Now, what do you say we give up on our little guy and go see if Aisha and Trent are doing a better job?"

I shrugged. "Why not?"

It wasn't as if my meager stabs at understanding the inner workings of an earthworm were going to make an iota of difference in my mother's life. I might as well throw in the scalpel and give up.

I lay back in the afternoon sun and propped my ice-cold can of diet Coke on my stomach. The fresh air smelled especially good after the overpowering odor of formaldehyde that had permeated Mr. Burgess's classroom. Nicole, Jane, and I had congregated on the lawn in front of Union High, where we were whiling away the few free minutes Nicole had before she had to leave for work at Claire's Boutique.

"I can't believe Matt asked you out for Saturday

night," Jane was saying. "I mean, of course I *believe* it since you're gorgeous and intelligent and funny. But given the fact that he's already going to the prom with one of the most popular girls in the senior class . . . this is a major coup."

"I guess so." I wished I could feel more excited about the upcoming date. But right now nothing seemed terribly exciting.

"I wonder if Sandra knows that you guys are going out this weekend," Jane continued. "If I were her, I'd be crushed."

Nicole waved her hand as if to dismiss the thought. "Come on—all Sandra cares about is the fact that she's got a hot date for her preprom photos. Why else would she have secured Matt *so* far in advance?" She raised her eyebrows. "Besides, I heard the only reason she asked him was to make her ex-boyfriend, Ed Polanski, jealous."

"Great," Jane said. "Then Christy has nothing to worry about. Matt is free and clear of obligation."

Nicole bit into a handful of Chee-tos. "I'll say this. Matt is extremely good-looking. He's not my type, but he's objectively outstanding in the blue-eyes-and-blond-hair department."

"Yeah, he is," I agreed. And he was. So what if he didn't want to talk about the possibilities of cancer research? Most high-school seniors were more interested in deciding where they were going to go to college than in obsessing over their mother's illness.

"And Matt is really easy to talk to," Jane added.

"He's not totally stuck-up like a lot of the other jocks."

"He's easy to be around," I confirmed. "But I don't know. . . . Do you think he's *deep?*"

"Deep?" Nicole crunched more Chee-tos, pondering the question. "Well . . . I wouldn't compare him to the Pacific Ocean. Then again, I don't think you're going to break your neck diving into the shallow end."

"It sounds like he's not afraid to let you know he cares," Jane added. "That's the important thing."

"Yeah . . . he does care," I responded. "As long as caring doesn't involve talking about my mother's illness. That subject totally freaks him out."

"You talked to him about that?" Nicole asked, sounding surprised. "You don't even talk to *us* about it."

"I didn't really *talk* to him about it. I just mentioned it a couple of times. That's all."

Even so, somewhere deep inside, it bothered me that Matt hadn't been more responsive to my casual references to my mom's cancer. Sure, I understood that it was an uncomfortable subject. But if *I* was willing to bring it up . . . then it seemed like a guy who was a potential boyfriend would want to hear what I had to say. Even *Jake* had been attentive to my need to vent. And he had the sensitivity of a droning, fly-bitten jolthead.

"Give him a chance," Nicole suggested. "It takes guys a while to open up." She paused. "At least, that's what I read in *Cosmopolitan.*"

I sat up and took several gulps from my can of soda. I thought of Matt's friendly smile and the warmth of his hand on my arm yesterday afternoon. Nicole and Jane were right. Matt was a great guy—any girl would consider herself lucky to have a date with him on Saturday night. I was going to have an awesome time . . . and I *certainly* wasn't going to let anything Jake Saunders had to say stand in the way of that awesome time. I couldn't wait!

The first thing I was aware of when I opened my eyes on Saturday morning was that I felt incredibly well rested. The second thing I was aware of was the sound of my dad whistling coming from somewhere downstairs.

I felt a sudden jolt of adrenaline and sat up ramrod straight in my bed. What was Dad doing up already? I always set my alarm clock so that I would be the first one awake, even on the weekends. Getting up early to make breakfast was a duty I took very seriously—it was my one consistent contribution to our family unit.

I looked over at the digital clock that sat on my nightstand. 10:30 A.M. I had overslept!

"Oh no!" I threw myself out of bed and reached for the robe I had thrown over my chaise lounge the night before. What had gone wrong? Had I accidentally turned off the alarm in my sleep?

I had my arms halfway into the sleeves of my robe when I heard a soft tap on my bedroom door.

"Dad, is that you?" I called. "I'm sorry it's so late—I don't know what happened."

"It's not Dad." The door opened, and I saw my mother smiling at me. "Good morning, sleepyhead," she said, her voice bright. "I told Dad to sneak in here this morning and turn off your alarm. We thought you deserved a few extra hours in bed."

"Oh . . . thanks." For a brief moment life felt almost normal again. Sleeping late. Dad whistling. Mom greeting me with the mug of herbal tea she was holding out to me. It was all so routine. Wonderfully, magically, awesomely routine.

"How do you feel, honey?" She walked into the room and over to the windows, where she opened the blinds to allow the sun in.

This morning Mom was wearing one of the three beautifully made wigs she had bought before she started chemotherapy. She had known her hair was going to fall out, and she had wanted to be prepared. But most days she was too tired to bother with them. She just wore a colorful scarf around her head and called herself Rhoda.

"I feel great," I responded, inhaling the delicious scent of the chamomile tea. "How are *you?*"

Mom sat down on my bed and pulled me next to her. "Christy, I woke up at six o'clock this morning, and I knew in my bones that this was going to be one of those precious, rare, *good* days."

I set the mug on the nightstand and wrapped my arms around my mother's waist. "Really, Mom?"

She nodded. "It's a reprieve. My body's out on furlough, so to speak."

I laughed. "How can you make jokes about this?" I asked, hugging her tight.

She kissed my forehead, then ran her fingers through my hair the way she had done when I was a little girl. "As long as I can laugh, this cancer hasn't gotten the best of me," she explained. "Christy, no matter what happens in the future, I never want you to forget the power of laughter."

"It's the best medicine, right?" I joked.

She squeezed me. "Right." I felt like my heart was going to burst, I was so happy to have my mom sitting on my bed and giving me advice. It was the best kind of Hallmark moment.

Finally my mother stood up. "I've got a brilliant idea," she announced.

"What is it?" I sipped my tea, thinking of all the "brilliant ideas" my mother had come up with before she got sick.

There was the picnic we went on one February afternoon. And our all-cotton-candy dinner when I was seven. Then there was the time that Mom decided at the last minute that she, Dad, and I should take a week off from work and school so that we could hike to the bottom of the Grand Canyon.

"Let's invite the Saunders family over for dinner tonight," she suggested. "We'll all stuff ourselves and then play a round of charades."

"But I—" *I have a date with Matt.*

Mom looked at me with a question in her eyes,

obviously wondering why I had stopped speaking midsentence. "What, sweetie? Do you have plans tonight?"

I shook my head. "No! I was just going to say that I think we should play Pictionary instead of charades."

"Then it's a plan," Mom declared. "We'll even let you and Jake be a team in the Pictionary game."

"Perfect." *Good-bye, date with Matt. Hello, evening with the urchin-snouted boar.*

But there was no date on earth that would make me give up spending a few hours with Mom when she was feeling this good. I hadn't seen her cheeks this bright in months. And if a family dinner with the Saunderses would make her happy, then I was going to put on a smile and be Jake's best friend for the duration of the evening. Anything to see her smile the way she was right now.

"Now all I have to do is call Molly and make sure their schedule is free . . . which I assume it is, since she's taken to bringing me a truckload of movie rentals every Saturday night."

"Can I make a call first?" I asked. "I just, uh, want to remind Nicole that she's got my history book."

"Of course, hon. Just come downstairs when you're off. Dad is making chocolate-chip pancakes."

As soon as she was gone, I picked up the receiver of the Minnie Mouse phone I had gotten for my thirteenth birthday. It was a slightly embarrassing possession for a seventeen-year-old, but hey, it did the job. I dialed Matt's number, which I had memorized the first day he had flirted with me in science class.

He answered the phone on the second ring. As soon as I heard Matt's voice, my heart sped up a little. This was the first time I had called him, which was a major step.

"Hey, it's Christy," I announced, hoping I sounded as cool and casual as I wanted to.

"Hi, Christy. How's my favorite lab partner?" His voice was low and sexy and made me a little bit sorry that we weren't going out tonight.

"I'm good," I responded. "Actually, I'm great."

"Does this mean you're psyched for tonight?" he asked. "I was just sitting here, looking at movie times."

I could picture Matt sitting at the kitchen table, a newspaper spread out in front of him. He was probably drinking a glass of milk and eating a huge bacon-and-eggs brunch. And he probably looked gorgeous, even if he was just wearing old sweatpants and a T-shirt.

I cleared my throat. "Unfortunately, I'm going to have to take a rain check," I told him. "You see, my mom is feeling really decent for the first time in, like, a long time . . . so we're having a kind of family dinner."

I didn't add that Jake was going to be there. I didn't want Matt to get the wrong impression. Guys could be weird that way.

"Oh." He was silent for a moment. "Did you

77

explain that you've got a date tonight? I mean, maybe you could get out of it."

I twisted the phone cord around my finger, pondering Matt's question. I could sort of understand where he was coming from. Most seniors in high school didn't do a victory dance when they discovered they were going to spend Saturday night with their parents.

But I was different. "I *want* to stay home with my parents," I explained. "The thing is, Matt, I don't get to spend a lot of so-called quality time with my mom. She doesn't feel all that well most of the time."

"Right. Sure, I understand," he said quickly. "Hey, it's no big deal. We'll do it another time."

"I'd like that." Maybe Matt didn't want to get into a major discussion about my mother's "good day," but that didn't mean he wasn't sensitive.

"I'll call you tomorrow," he promised. Once again Matt's alluring voice made me feel a twinge of regret that I wasn't going to get to sit next to him in a darkened movie theater tonight. Instead I would be trading glares with Jake.

As I hung up the phone, I was already scanning the titles of the cookbooks I had started to collect. After the dozen or so pancakes I was going to eat for breakfast, I planned to prepare a veritable feast. I was going to make sure that tonight was an evening none of us would ever forget.

Eight

Jake

"IT SMELLS GREAT in here," I announced on Saturday night as I walked through the swinging door that led to the Redmonds' kitchen. "I feel like I'm walking into the kitchen of a five-star restaurant."

Christy looked up from the pan in which she was sautéing some kind of green vegetable. "Hey, I didn't hear you all come in."

I wasn't surprised. Judging from the number of dirty pots and pans in the sink and the five cookbooks on the kitchen counter, it looked like Christy had been so deep into making dinner that she probably wouldn't have noticed an earthquake.

"We got here about five minutes ago," I informed her. "Your mom looks great."

Christy nodded, beaming. "I know. She's been

79

like this all day. It's . . . I can't even explain how great it is."

She didn't have to explain. The expression on Christy's face said it all. Her eyes were shining, her cheeks were flushed, and her smile was so big that it seemed to take up her entire face. I couldn't help grinning back. This kind of mood was infectious.

"Thanks for coming tonight, Jake," Christy said quietly. "I'm sure there were a million things you would have rather done with your Saturday night than come here to hang out with me and my family."

"Nah," I said, shrugging. "All I had to look forward to was me, a bag of microwave popcorn, and the World Wrestling Federation on TV."

Okay, that wasn't exactly true. I had been planning for the last two weeks to go to a baseball game tonight with two of my best friends, Bill Feldman and John Hernandez. But as soon as my mom had told me that Rose was feeling up to having our family over for dinner, I knew I was going to be bagging my plans for the game.

I wasn't stupid. I knew there was the possibility that this was the last time our families would ever spend an evening together. Maybe hanging out with Christy wasn't first on my list of fun things to do now, but we'd had a lot of awesome times together as kids. And I knew that it meant a lot to my mom to have me there, rounding out the picture of two happy families.

Tonight I wanted to recapture the warmth and

security of childhood, when the only thing I worried about was whether or not I could have another bowl of ice cream and if it would be warm enough Sunday afternoon to play softball. I just hoped that Christy could experience that same sense of well-being. She needed it even more than I did.

"So are you going to stand there and stare at me, or are you going to make yourself useful?" Christy asked.

I grabbed an apron that was hanging on a hook next to the oven. It wasn't until I had already put it on that I realized it read Women Who Cook Know How to Turn Up the Heat.

Christy giggled. "Don't worry. I won't tell any of your friends about this particular fashion choice."

"If you do, I'll deny everything," I joked.

I walked over to Christy and peered over her shoulder. She had four different pots and pans on the stove, each of which contained something I couldn't identify. Of course, my idea of cooking a meal consisted of heating up a can of tomato soup or dialing Pizza Hut.

"So, what are we making?" I asked.

"We're preparing baked Brie with pecans, orange tarragon chicken, almond rice, and for dessert, toffee cookie diamonds." Christy was pointing to the various pans as she spoke.

I whistled. "I had no idea you'd turned into such a gourmand. Last I remember, the only things you could cook were hot dogs and packaged tortellini."

She laughed. "I've come a long way, baby." She pointed to the stack of cookbooks. "See those? All mine."

I was impressed. "I wouldn't have pegged you as the stay-in-the-kitchen type," I commented. "It seems so 1950s."

She arched an eyebrow. "Gee! Thanks." She set a bowl of almonds in front of me and handed me a knife. "Here. Chop these."

Good going, Jake, I reprimanded myself. Now that we were finally having a pleasant exchange, I had managed to put not only my foot in my mouth—but the sock and penny loafer I was wearing as well.

"I—I . . . uh . . . that didn't come out right," I stammered. "I'm, like, totally wowed by this new-found cooking ability."

I chopped an almond, hoping my faux pas wasn't going to send us into a full-on verbal battle. I just wasn't in the mood to tear Christy to shreds with witty comebacks. Or be torn to shreds *myself,* for that matter.

"Don't worry about it," she said, pulling a tray of chicken breasts out of the refrigerator. "To tell you the truth, the only reason I've been cooking so much is to feel like I'm doing something to help out." She paused. "And it helps somehow . . . it's sort of therapy, I guess."

"I really admire the way you're dealing with all of this," I said quietly, concentrating on the small pile of diced almonds growing in front of me. "I don't know how I would handle it if my mom got sick."

Christy sighed. "I pray to God you'll never have to know how you'd handle it," she responded. "It's not something I would wish on my worst enemy."

"Is that what I am?" I asked. "Your worst enemy?"

She looked at me for a long moment. "Nah. You're just a pain in the butt."

I popped an almond in my mouth. "Right back at you, kid."

Christy put the chicken in the oven. Then she took out a bag of brown sugar and carefully measured out a cup. She was a veritable dynamo. I stopped chopping my almonds and watched with fascination as Christy sped around the kitchen, mixing, whisking, and beating. She was like Julia Child, only a lot better looking.

"I have a proposal," Christy announced, cracking an egg into a clear glass bowl.

Hastily I turned back to the almonds. "What's that?"

"I propose that we don't mention anything related to illness, especially cancer, for the rest of the night," she announced. "For the next few hours I'm going to try to forget that my mom is sick."

I set down the knife and looked Christy in the eyes. "Can you really do that?" I asked. "Can you forget?"

She gave a smile that was so brave, it made my heart ache. "I can try, Jake."

"Count me in," I told her. "I won't even sneeze. I promise."

She examined my almond pile, then nodded approvingly. "Looks good."

"Thanks." It was the closest Christy had come to giving me a compliment since the sixth grade.

"Think you can move on to boiling a pot of water for rice?" Christy asked. "I've got to get the rice ready."

I squinted. "Let's see. . . . Boiling water . . . How do I do that again?"

She groaned. "I'll walk you through it step by step."

As I filled a giant pot with water, I couldn't help thinking that I was experiencing something that people might describe as "fun." Since our usual icy rapport was thawing out, tonight really did feel like old times. And I liked it. I liked it a lot.

"I'd like to propose a toast," Mr. Redmond announced as we were all finishing our chicken and rice. He lifted his glass. "To family, friends, and love."

As he spoke of love, Mr. Redmond turned to his wife and gazed into her eyes. The way they looked at each other almost brought tears to my eyes. I glanced at Christy out of the corner of my eye and saw that she was also studying her parents.

"I love you, Bobby," Rose said to her husband. "I love all of you . . . so much."

I knew with my gut that Christy was looking

into the future and wondering how she and her dad would go on if the worst happened. I wished I could reach out and hold her hand . . . but I couldn't. It wasn't what she needed right now.

"Hey, enough of the mushy stuff," I said. "How about a toast to the chef? This is the best meal I've had in months!"

My mom laughed. "Is that a hint about my cooking?"

Mrs. Redmond winked at Mom. "I think he's a little biased."

"You're an excellent chef," my dad told Christy as he patted his stomach. "I ate way too much. The meal was truly fabulous, Christy."

I saw Christy blush. "I just hope the toffee cookie diamonds come out all right," she commented. "I think I burned the crust."

"They'll be wonderful, Christy," my dad said quickly. "And I'm sure Jake will eat about a dozen of them to prove it."

Rose leaned back in her seat and looked at Christy and me with a sort of beatific gaze in her eyes. "I can't wait to see the two of you on prom night next weekend," she mused. "I know it's silly that I'm so romantic about a high-school dance, but I can't help myself. When Bobby and I went to *our* prom, it was the night he told me he loved me for the very first time."

Beside me Christy was shifting uncomfortably in her seat. "Mom, come on. . . ."

"I'm sorry, sweetie. But surely you can indulge

your old mom when she wants to bask in the reflected glow of young love."

Suddenly I realized that Mrs. Redmond was under the impression that Christy and I were more than prom dates. She thought we were on the verge of, like, a major relationship. Under normal circumstances I would have no doubt that Christy would disabuse her mom of such a crazy idea. Under *normal* circumstances she would probably have loved nothing more than to go on for hours to her mom about what a jerk I was.

But right now I figured Christy would do just about anything to make her mom smile. And if that included letting her mom believe that she and I were an item . . . it was my job to keep the illusion going.

I took a deep breath, preparing to take the plunge. And then I did it. I casually slung my arm around Christy's shoulders. *Please don't humiliate me by slapping away my hand,* I thought.

When she didn't immediately elbow me in the ribs, I started to relax a little. "I can't wait for the prom either," I announced. "Christy is going to be the most beautiful girl at the dance."

That much was true. Despite her many personality flaws, there was no disputing the fact that Christy would be outstanding in her prom dress. I could envision her creamy skin and red lips and soft, shiny hair. . . . *Whoa. Stop. Rewind.* This was Christy who I was thinking about.

So it was Christy. But I was a guy. I was human.

I wasn't going to pretend to myself that I didn't like the sensation of having my arm around her. It felt pretty great, actually. *It's only taken me five years to get another chance to put my arm around her,* I thought. *That must be a world record.*

"Jake and I will dance the night away," Christy said to the group. "It'll be just like a movie."

Then she leaned in close to me. "Just like a *bad* movie," she whispered.

Absurdly, Christy's stinging remark was like getting a knife in the chest. I quickly removed my arm and put my hands in my lap. So much for Ms. Nice Girl. Christy was just being nice to me to please her mother. I should have known.

Yes, I *should* have known. But for that one second, when I had thought that she actually *meant* we were going to dance the night away, my heart had thumped.

You're insane, Jake, I told myself. *You don't even like this girl.* I had been caught up in the moment. That was all. It could happen to anyone.

"A *really* bad movie," I whispered back to let her know that I was in on the "joke."

Still, the magic of the night was gone. When Christy left the table to get the toffee cookie diamonds, I found that I had lost my appetite.

Nine

Christy

"I HOPE THERE'S more to the plot than blowing up buildings and chase scenes," I said to Matt as we settled into our seats at the movie theater on Sunday afternoon. "Special effects only carry a movie so far."

"I'm sure there will also be a beautiful blond girl with an attitude," Matt assured me. "There's always a love interest." He paused. "Of course, *I* prefer brunettes."

"Thanks, Matt. I appreciate that." I held out the giant tub of buttered popcorn we had bought, and he took a handful. "And thanks for calling this morning. I didn't expect you to be so prompt with my rain check."

"Life is short," Matt commented. "You've got to go for it." Then he looked at me and sort of choked on his popcorn. "Uh, sorry. I didn't mean . . ."

I reached over and squeezed his hand. "That's okay. I know you weren't referring to my mom."

He gulped. "Um, would you like some Milk Duds?" He held out the box.

I took a handful and bit into them. "But you're right," I said when I was finally able to swallow the chewy mass. "My mom's sickness has taught me how important it is to enjoy life. Then again, it's also made it *harder* to enjoy life. I mean, I'm sitting here with you, but part of me is still at home, wondering how my mom is feeling."

Matt nudged me. "Uh, they're dimming the lights. I think the previews are about to start."

"Oh . . . right." I turned away from Matt and settled more comfortably into my seat. But as the theater darkened, I knew I wouldn't really be paying attention to the movie.

When I had woken up this morning, I had been filled with hope that Mom was going to have another great day. I had even started to think about plans for tonight, and next week, and next month. But when I brought in her breakfast, I realized immediately that no miracle had taken place. Mom was already awake and reaching for one of her pain pills when I walked into the room. The respite had ended.

Then again, she had eaten almost all of the strawberry-topped waffles I had made for breakfast. Maybe the pain she had felt this morning was one of those fleeting things that would be gone by the time I got home from the movies.

On the screen there were dizzying images of an exploding planet, a beautiful woman running down a long, dark corridor, and a beefy actor scaling the side of a skyscraper. It looked exactly like the preview for every other movie that had come out in the last five years. Boring.

"I can't wait to see this," Matt whispered to me. "We'll have to make it a date."

"Uh, yeah." I wondered if for every action flick I saw with Matt, he would accompany me to an indie film. Huh. Probably not.

The previews ended, and the movie began. As I watched the titles roll across the screen, I thought about last night. It had been so amazing to see my mother feeling like her old self. . . . It was almost as if she had been reborn.

And Jake. I hadn't been able to get him out of my head all day. I had forgotten what it was like to hang out with him minus the acrimonious comments. Part of me had felt like suggesting, *Hey, why don't we let the past go and pick up our friendship where it ended—that fateful night when we were thirteen?*

In fact, there was even a tiny part of me that had wanted more. When I had felt his arm around me, a tingle had traveled from my shoulders to the tips of my fingers. Why? *Just residual emotions from preadolescence,* I told myself, shifting now so that my shoulder was touching Matt's.

But I *had* been impressed by how relaxed Jake

had been around my mom. Even Nicole and Jane felt a little nervous about how to act and what to say in front of a person with cancer.

Of course, Matt would probably never meet my mother. First of all, I hadn't stopped her from believing that there might be something going on between Jake and me. Why confuse that issue with Matt? Second, I knew without having to ask that Matt would *definitely* be uncomfortable about Mom's illness. He just couldn't deal with it. Not like Jake.

Don't do that! I told myself. Why did I keep comparing and contrasting Jake and Matt? One had nothing to do with the other. And the fact that I had felt sparks when Jake touched me, whereas I felt only a warm fuzzy when Matt touched me, meant nothing.

In the darkness of the theater I slipped my hand into Matt's. I was positive that once we knew each other better, there would be sparks aplenty. How could there not be? Unlike Jake, Matt was the perfect guy.

I held my pillow over my head, trying in vain to block out the sounds coming from my parents' bedroom. It was almost two o'clock in the morning, and I couldn't sleep. I had woken up from a deep sleep almost an hour ago to the sound of Mom whimpering in pain in her bedroom.

Her soft, muffled crying made my heart feel like it had been shattered into a million shards of glass. I knew it was equally painful for my father. I could hear his gentle, murmuring voice as he spoke. He was probably rubbing her shoulders and whispering to her that everything was going to be all right.

But it wasn't. I was starting to know in my gut that nothing was ever going to be all right again. The feeling had started the minute I arrived home from my date with Matt. Dad had been sitting on the sofa in the living room, just sort of staring at the wall. He hadn't even noticed that I had come inside.

I had walked over to Dad and tapped him on the shoulder. "Is everything okay?" I asked.

He didn't nod or shake his head or say anything at all. He just blinked, as if I had woken him from a deep sleep. I had never seen him look so defeated.

"Dad?" I asked, louder this time. "Is Mom okay?"

Finally he reached up and took my hand. "She had to increase her pain medication, hon."

I hadn't asked him any more questions. I hadn't wanted to. I was too afraid of what the answers might be. I had simply gone upstairs, kissed my mother as she lay sleeping, and locked myself in my bedroom. Then I had buried myself in homework, resolutely pushing away the image of my father's forlorn face.

But now that it was the middle of the night and the house was dark and quiet—except for the soft sounds coming from my parents' bedroom—I couldn't stop the thoughts that were whirling through my brain.

The dark night of the soul, I thought. My mom was sick. She had cancer. Unless a miracle happened, she was going to die.

"She's going to die." I had never said the words aloud before. I wasn't sure if I had ever even *thought* the words. They were the worst, most devastating, most terrifying words in the universe.

Save her, I thought. *If there's anyone out there, I'm begging you. Please, please save my mother.*

I almost wished Mom hadn't felt so good yesterday. Her brief reprieve from her illness made the reality of it even more painful than it had been before. I wished I had never seen what I had interpreted as a light at the end of the tunnel. Now the tunnel was bleaker, darker, and more depressing than it had been before.

And I was exhausted. I was tired of being strong. I was tired of holding in my emotions so that nobody would know that I felt like I was slipping into a black hole. I felt like I was about to burst.

Suddenly the house was completely still. Thankfully, both of my parents had apparently fallen asleep. It was the only time when they didn't have to think about what was going on around us. I was sure that in her dreams, my mom was as healthy as she had been when she was eighteen, walking into her senior prom with my dad on her arm.

But I was wide awake. I felt like I would never sleep again. "I have to talk to somebody," I realized, speaking aloud.

I couldn't go another minute without *telling*

someone about what I was going through. If I didn't, I was going to lose my mind.

I switched on the light next to my bed and picked up the receiver of the Minnie Mouse phone. I would call Nicole. She had her own telephone line, and I knew she wouldn't mind if I woke her up in the middle of the night.

Then I set the phone down again. I knew that both Nicole and Jane would be more than happy to listen to me vent. But where was I going to start? It had been my decision not to talk to them much about my mom's illness. As a result, they didn't know a lot about it. I wanted to speak to someone who *understood*. Or came as close to understanding as someone who wasn't going through this could.

Jake. I don't know what made me think of him, of all people. Maybe it was the fact that he had known my mother practically since the day he was born. Maybe it was because he had just seen her. Or because his mother was Mom's best friend. Or because he was the only one who had asked me about her condition lately.

Maybe it's because he's been there for you before, I thought. I would never forget the day that we had put our dog, Pepper, to sleep. I had been in the sixth grade, and when I got home from school, Mom had told me that Pepper had been hit by a car. The vet had done everything he could, but if Pepper lived, she would be in pain for the rest of her life.

Mom had taken me onto her lap, and she had

talked to me like a grown-up for the first time in my life. Together we had decided that the most humane thing to do was put Pepper out of her misery. We had gone to the veterinarian's office, and I had held Pepper while she died.

Up to that point, it had been the worst day of my life. Afterward I had been inconsolable. I was sure we had made the wrong decision. What if they discovered a cure for whatever was wrong with Pepper? What if she had *wanted* to live despite the pain?

That night I hadn't been able to sleep. Once I had cried all of my tears, I realized that I wanted to talk to someone who had known Pepper as well as I had. And that person was Jake. He had been there when I taught her to fetch and to sit. He had helped me dress her up as Yoda one Halloween night. He loved her just like I did.

I had sneaked out of the house, terrified that my parents would wake up and ground me for a lifetime. Then I had sprinted down to Jake's house and thrown pebbles at the window that used to be his bedroom. He had woken up and let me inside, no questions asked. I had stayed for two hours, and when I left, I knew that I would be able to sleep.

I got out of my bed now, feeling like I was running on autopilot. I picked up the pink scrunchie sitting on my nightstand and put my hair back into a loose ponytail. Then I slipped into the jeans I had left lying next to my bed and pulled a T-shirt out of my drawer. There was only one person in the world

I wanted to talk to right now. And it was the very last person I would have ever expected it to be . . .

Outside, the air was cool. There wasn't a cloud in the sky; instead it was filled with millions of stars. I jogged down the block, living completely in the moment. If I stopped to think about what I was doing, I knew that I would turn around and go back to my house, where I would sit up all night, chewing on my fingernails.

I slowed to a walk as I approached the Saunderses' house. I knew that Jake had moved down to the basement. I had heard my mom and Molly talking about it last year—something about Jake "needing more privacy now that his hormones are raging."

I crept to the side of the house. There it was. The front basement window. *Am I really going to do this?* I asked myself. But I had to. I needed to talk, and Jake was the only person who would be real with me. He wouldn't go overboard with condolences or try to pretend that he knew what I was going through. He would just be . . . him. Like he had been the night that Pepper died.

I rapped on the small basement window three times. Then I waited. And waited. I knocked again. *I'll go back,* I decided. *He's sound asleep.* And this was a totally insane idea anyway. By tomorrow I would be fine. I would build back up my defenses overnight, and I would cope.

I started to turn away from the window.

"Christy? Is that you?" I heard his voice behind me, coming from inside the house.

I turned around. He had opened the window, and he was staring straight at me. "Uh, yeah," I whispered. "I just . . . never mind. Go back to bed."

He shook his head. "No. Go around back. I'll let you in through the basement door."

"Thanks." As I headed toward the back of the house, I hoped I was doing the right thing.

Jake was my archfoe, my sparring partner, my surly, spur-galled foot-licker. But was he my *friend*? I reached the door, my heart pounding. *You're about to find out, Christy.*

Ten

Christy

"COME INSIDE," JAKE said as soon as he opened the basement door that led to his bedroom.

I walked into the house and followed Jake down a small, narrow hallway. At the end of the hallway was the door that opened into Jake's bedroom. Actually, it was more like an apartment, complete with a sitting area, a Ping-Pong table, and a minifridge in the corner.

"Is everything okay?" Jake asked anxiously. He was wearing pajama bottoms and a T-shirt, and his hair looked like it had been through a tornado. "Is it your mom?"

I flopped onto an old, half-stuffed beanbag chair. "She's fine. I mean, no, she's not fine. She hasn't been fine for a long, long time. But for some crazy reason I've been going around telling anyone who asks that she *is*. And now I can't do that anymore. . . ." I sighed deeply, sinking farther into the giant beanbag. "Oh, man, I don't even know why I'm here."

Jake perched on the edge of an old couch. It was the same one that had been in their living room before Mrs. Saunders had gone on a Martha Stewart–style redecorating binge. "Christy—"

"I'm going to leave," I interrupted. "This was a stupid idea."

What had I been *thinking?* I had woken up Jake in the middle of the night so that he could sit there and listen to me, probably his least-favorite person in the world, moan and groan about my problems. It was ridiculous. I pushed my hands against the floor and heaved myself off the beanbag.

Jake stood up and grabbed my arm. "Christy, listen to me for *one* second."

"What?" I couldn't exactly refuse to hear what the guy had to say. Not after I had woken him up (probably from a dream about Jennifer Love Hewitt or Cindy Crawford).

"I think you should stay for a while. I mean, you obviously came here for a reason. And now you're up, and I'm up . . . and, well, we might as well talk."

I sort of fell onto the sofa. My legs just kind of gave out from under me. I didn't say anything at first. I gazed around Jake's room, taking in every detail. There were trophies, sports posters, and CDs everywhere. A miniature basketball hoop was attached to

100

one of the walls, and his mom's old StairMaster (which Jake seemed to be using as a clothes-hanging device) was in the corner.

It was all so typically *male* that I realized suddenly that this was the first time since sixth grade that I had been alone with a guy in his room. Of course, since that guy was Jake, it didn't really count. My gaze fell on the peewee swimming trophy he had won in fifth grade. I had been on the other end of the lane, cheering him to victory. After the meet both of our families had gone to Jon's Pizza for a celebration.

"Everything used to be so simple," I said finally. "Swim meets, pizza, minigolf . . ."

Jake sat down beside me. "Yeah. Sometimes I wish I didn't have to grow up. I mean, I want to go to college and become independent—but I miss the time that I could fix any problem with a hot-fudge sundae or a trip to the arcade."

"Remember the time we ran away from home together?" I asked.

Jake laughed. "I don't know how far we thought we were going to get with two ham sandwiches, a package of Oreo cookies, and four dollars."

"Hey, we made it all the way to McDonald's," I pointed out. "I think that was the best Happy Meal I ever had."

"And then your mom showed up with a suitcase," Jake continued. "She said that as long as we were running away, she was going to come with us."

I giggled. "To tell you the truth, I think she got

that technique from an old *Brady Bunch* episode."

"It worked," Jake responded. "You were so worried that your dad was going to be lonely all by himself that you insisted we abandon our plan to move to Disney World."

I sighed. "My mom was really something, wasn't she?"

"She still is." Jake scooped up a Nerf basketball and tossed it in the direction of the hoop. It hit the rim, fell to the floor, then rolled in our direction.

"I don't know what we're going to do without her," I whispered. "I'm so scared, Jake. If I even think about the worst-case scenario, I feel like I'm going to completely fall apart."

Jake picked up the basketball again and squeezed it into a tight, orange ball. "It's okay if you fall apart, Christy. You're entitled."

I took the ball from him and threw it. It swished through the hoop. "Two points," I declared.

"Really, Christy, you don't need to pretend that everything is okay. There are a lot of people around who would love a chance to lend you a shoulder."

I shook my head. "I have to be strong. I don't want my parents to know how terrified I am." I paused, again thinking of the way my dad was sitting in the living room tonight, staring into space. "They need me to have a smile on my face, Jake. It's all they've got right now."

"It's at times like these that it's rough to be an only child," Jake commented. "If you had a sister or a brother, maybe you wouldn't feel so compelled to keep a stiff upper lip, as they say."

I laughed softly. "You know what's weird? You're probably the closest thing I have to a sibling." I paused. "Maybe that's why I'm here."

"We were sort of like a brother and a sister when we were little," Jake agreed. He got up and grabbed the basketball. "We used to squabble like two kids stuck in the backseat of a car during a long road trip."

I nodded. "I loved all that bickering when I was young. It made me feel . . . I don't know . . . safe somehow."

Jake threw the ball, and it went through the hoop. "Two points. We're tied." He reached for the ball again, then handed it to me. "We're still pretty fantastic in the bickering department."

"True." I tossed the basketball. It didn't land anywhere near the hoop this time. "But it feels different now."

Jake sighed, then shifted so that his back was against the plush arm of the sofa. "I guess hormones got in the way. We hit puberty and *bam*, everything changed."

I grinned. "You know, we never should have gone on that stupid date. It was the beginning of the end of a beautiful friendship."

My heart skipped a beat. I couldn't believe I had just mentioned that taboo subject. Neither Jake nor I had directly referred to our date since that awful night. I had been so caught up in our conversation that the comment had slipped out before my internal censor weeded it out.

"Man, that was a disaster," Jake said with a laugh. "I was so nervous that my palms produced about a liter of sweat that night."

"Same here." How could I forget? When Jake had tried to hold my hand, I had yanked it away as if he were on fire.

"Really?" Jake asked. He attempted to spin the basketball on the tip of his finger. "You seemed so calm, cool, and collected. I never would have guessed that you were the least bit nervous."

"Ha!" I exclaimed. "Are you *kidding?* That was, like, the biggest night of my life. It was the first time I ever wore lip gloss."

"I warranted lip gloss?" Jake teased. "Wow. I never knew."

"Well, if you hadn't been so busy antagonizing the waiter, maybe you would have noticed that my lips were incredibly red and sensuous for a thirteen-year-old."

Jake set down the Nerf ball between us. "I noticed," he said quietly. "Trust me, I noticed."

I shifted so that I was facing Jake. And I looked at him. I mean, I really *looked* at him. He appeared to be the same boy I had built forts with in his backyard. But he was also someone totally different. He had broad shoulders, and I could see the muscles in his chest lurking somewhere under his T-shirt. Funny. I had never noticed what a square jaw he had . . . or the way his hair brushed his ears in just the right way.

I became acutely aware of two facts. The first was that I hadn't felt this close to another person in ages—not since my mother had received her initial diagnosis, and I had started to pull away from Jane and Nicole. Just being able to really *talk* to someone made me feel like I could start cracking away at the wall I had built around my heart.

The second fact was even more mind-blowing. Out of nowhere, I had become aware of Jake's presence in an entirely different way. I was conscious of his body, his arms, his strong hands resting lightly on the basketball.

And I couldn't take my eyes off his lips. They were full and red and exactly the kind of lips that girls dreamed of kissing. I felt thirteen all over again . . . only not. Now I was seventeen, and kissing wasn't just something I had read about in books. I had done it. And I could imagine what it would be like with Jake.

"Are you wearing lip gloss right now?" Jake asked, his voice so husky that it sent chills down my spine.

He was staring into my eyes. My body felt like it was turning to liquid as I nodded. "Um, a little. It's left over from this afternoon."

He reached out and brushed my hair away from my face. "It looks nice." A vein in his forehead throbbed as if it had a life of its own.

"Thanks." My voice was so low that it was barely a whisper.

Jake leaned closer to me, and I found myself responding to him like a magnet. I moved closer to him, my eyes falling again to his lips.

Time seemed to stand still, and I realized that at this moment, I wanted to kiss Jake Saunders more than I ever could have dreamed possible.

Eleven

Jake

ALL OF THE blood in my body had rushed to my head, and I felt like I was about to faint. At the same time every one of my five senses was hyperalert as I continued to stare into Christy's eyes.

My mouth was so close to her lips that I could practically taste them. It was as if the dream I'd had the other night was coming to life. But this moment was even more intense than it had been in the dream. Because now I could detect the slight scent of apple from the shampoo Christy used on her shiny, dark hair. It was intoxicating.

I'm about to kiss Christy Redmond. For the first time ever, I was aware that this was something I had wanted to do for a long, long time.

I closed my eyes and leaned even closer, closing

the tiny amount of space that was still between us. But I didn't find her lips with mine. There was just empty space where her mouth had been.

My eyes popped open. Christy was on the other side of the couch, as far away as she could get from me. She had jerked away at the last possible second. And she was still staring at me—but now her eyes were flashing with anger.

"Christy, what's the matter?" I felt like the proverbial rug had been ripped out from under my feet.

She scowled. "I don't need your *pity* kiss, Jake." She stood up and crossed her arms protectively against her chest. "I should never have come here."

"What are you *talking* about?" I yelled—as loudly as I could without running the risk of waking up my parents.

"I'm out of here." Christy didn't give me a chance to say anything else.

She spun around and strode toward the door of my bedroom. "Just wait—"

But it was too late. She had started running. By the time I reached the door, she had already fled down the hallway and out the door that led to the backyard. I had to let her go. I couldn't exactly chase a girl down the block in the middle of the night.

Instead I ran back into my room and stood by the window, where I had a view of the street. I watched as Christy sprinted down the block and slipped safely back into her house.

"What just happened here?" I asked myself, gazing at the sofa.

I was confused, frustrated, and annoyed. Christy had *wanted* me to kiss her. I was sure of it. What was her *deal?* I had never met someone who ran so hot and cold.

I bent over and picked up the basketball. Then I threw it as hard as I could against the wall, wishing I could vent some of my pent-up emotion.

Had Christy intentionally come over to get me all riled up so that she could throw it back in my face? It didn't seem possible. . . . Then again, two hours ago I wouldn't have thought it possible that I'd be woken up in the middle of the night by my sparring partner either.

"Nothing makes sense anymore." I moaned, flopping onto my bed.

I felt terrible that Christy's mother was sick, but I also resented the way Christy was treating me. Just because she was going through a traumatic time didn't mean she could use me as an emotional punching bag. I was a human being with feelings! Not that Christy had the power to *hurt* me. I didn't even like her. I didn't! The nonkiss had been . . . what?

A mistake. A moment of weakness. A severe error in judgment. I was *glad* Christy had pulled away. I would have regretted the kiss the second that it ended, if not sooner. I should consider myself lucky that it never happened.

I reached out and flipped off the switch of the overhead light. Unfortunately, I was going to have to wake up in a few short hours. Tomorrow was going to be a complete wash. But it wasn't going to be anywhere near as miserable as prom night. If the way tonight had gone was any indication, the dance was going to be nothing short of a nightmare.

"Jake! Are you awake down there?" My mother's voice at the top of the stairs, combined with the buzz of the alarm clock, jolted me out of a deep sleep.

I turned over and banged my fist against the alarm clock. "I'm up!" I yelled back.

Groggily I slid out of bed and headed directly for a hot shower. As I passed the couch, last night came flooding back to me. Had I been dreaming, or had Christy really shown up at my door in the middle of the night?

Then I noticed a pink ponytail holder lying on the floor next to the sofa. Yep. She had been here, all right. So it was all real. Her showing up. Our conversation. The kiss. *The kiss that never happened,* I amended to myself.

In the bathroom I turned on the shower full blast and stepped inside. As the hot water poured over my head, I mulled over the events of last night. Christy had been incredibly upset when she had arrived—obviously. She never would have come over if she hadn't been totally desperate for someone—anyone—to talk to.

Maybe I had overreacted when I had been so angry that she bolted without a word of explanation. It wasn't as if I knew how *I* would behave under similar circumstances. If my mom were as sick as Rose was . . . I didn't even want to think about what I might do.

I stepped out of the shower and wrapped a towel around my waist. I felt considerably more awake—but I also felt guilty. Christy hadn't been the one in the wrong last night. I had been.

She had been totally vulnerable, and she had trusted me. She had shared her fears with me. I was sure she hadn't told anyone else about her need to be strong on the outside no matter what happened. And I was fairly certain that she hadn't voiced her worst fear of all to anyone else . . . that her mother wasn't going to beat this thing.

I wiped away the steam-covered mirror and gazed at my foggy reflection. "You're a jerk," I told myself.

Rule number one in the code of chivalry was never to take advantage of a girl when she was feeling vulnerable. I hadn't *intended* to take advantage of Christy, but maybe it had been wrong of me to try to kiss her under the circumstances.

True, she had seemed as ready for the kiss as I had been. But at the last second she must have come to her senses and remembered that she didn't even *like* me. *I'll apologize,* I decided.

Everything had been so mixed up last night that at this point I wasn't sure who had been right and who had been wrong. But one thing had become clear. My mom had been right. Christy needed friends right now. And I wanted to be in that category.

I wanted to be there for Christy . . . for old times' sake, if nothing else.

★　　★　　★

I spent most of my lunch period searching for Christy so that I could give her a timely apology. Finally, ten minutes before the bell was going to ring for next period, I found her sitting at a corner table in the library. She was eating an apple and staring at her calculus textbook.

"Hey." I stood in front of the table and waited for her to look up from the math problems.

"Jake, what are you doing here?" she asked, sounding extremely suspicious.

So much for crying on my shoulder. "I, uh, wanted to talk about last night," I explained. "I mean, it was pretty weird."

Cut to the chase, I ordered myself. *Just tell the girl you're sorry.*

She laughed. "Forget about last night."

"What?" I had been ready for just about anything. But *laughter?*

Christy set down her apple and folded her hands together on top of the table. "Listen, Jake, last night I had a bad case of temporary insanity."

"You did." I wasn't sure if I was making a statement or posing a question. Christy always had the effect of throwing me completely off balance.

She nodded. "It was late; I couldn't sleep." She gave me a tight, mean (in my opinion) smile. "Consider it an insomnia-provoked dementia."

Showing up at my house might have been a little out of the ordinary. But I didn't think I would have labeled the act *demented.* "Well, whatever it was, I just wanted to let you know that I—"

"Save it," Christy interrupted. "Whatever you're about to say is totally irrelevant. Because we're just going to pretend that it never happened." She raised her eyebrows and gave me a challenging stare. "End. Of. Story."

So she wasn't looking for an apology. Okay. Fine. I was still going to give the friend thing one more shot. For my mom. For Rose. For Christy.

"End of story. I understand," I echoed. "But I wanted you to know that I'm here for you. That's all."

"Thank you." But Christy's voice conveyed anything *but* gratitude. "I'll keep that in mind." She glanced back at her textbook. "Now, do you mind? I'm trying to get my homework done before class."

Nice, I thought. I turned my back on Christy and strode across the library. Our conversation certainly hadn't been worth giving up my lunch for. In fact, it had been a complete waste of time.

From now on I was going to stay as far away from Christy as I could. That was obviously what she wanted—and that's what she was going to get. End. Of. Story.

Twelve

Christy

"**I** HAVE TO find him," Nicole said for the thousandth time on Monday afternoon. "That's all there is to it."

Nicole had gotten herself into quite a quandary. She'd told two members of the Jerk Brigade (our name for the nastiest clique at Union High) that a certain hot guy was her prom date—a guy she'd never even met! And now she had to track down the guy and beg him to be her date.

The three of us were sharing a basket of fries at the food court in the mall. Nicole was continuing to obsess about finding her man, and Jane and I were mostly nodding.

"The prom is five days away, and I've got *nothing*." Nicole moaned.

"Christy and I will keep looking, won't we?"

Jane announced, nudging me in the ribs.

"Yeah, of course we will," I answered automatically. Jane and I had been with Nicole when she'd pointed out the total stranger to the Jerk Brigade.

Unfortunately, I knew I wasn't going to be all that much help. I had barely seen the guy. My mind, as usual, had been on my mom—not on the cute guy who'd taken his kid sister shopping for a dress at the shop Nicole works in.

"We should check out all of the kids' stores," Nicole suggested. "After all, the last time we actually *saw* the guy, he was with his little sister. And we should get started on checking out the other local high schools."

I nodded absently. I wanted to concentrate on Nicole's problem. I really did. But while she was focused on public humiliation, I was worried about my own, *private* humiliation.

I couldn't stop thinking about last night. I had managed to act nonchalant when Jake had found me hiding in the library today, but inside I had been a mess. When I woke up this morning, I had hoped that the whole scene at Jake's had been some kind of surreal nightmare.

Then I had noticed that I was still wearing the T-shirt I had put on to go over to his house. I hadn't been dreaming. This was real. I had made a total fool of myself, and there was nothing I could do about it.

What was I thinking? I wondered for around the millionth time today. The more times I went over last night in my head, the more embarrassed I was. Going over to Jake's house in the middle of the night had been worse than desperate. It was pathetic!

I shouldn't have let myself get to a place where I would do something so pitiable. I should have been able to stay strong. Or if I simply *couldn't* hold in my emotions another second, Jake was the last person I should have turned to. I was like a thorn in his side—and I had been for years.

I should have called Jane or Nicole or written in my nonexistent diary or called the Psychic Hotline or talked to myself in the mirror. *Anything* would have been better than the dead-of-night call I had inflicted upon poor, unsuspecting Jake.

I'm never going to blubber on Jake's shoulder again, I vowed to myself. I would have to deal with him at the prom on Saturday night, but after that, I was going to steer clear of him as much as I possibly could.

At least I had managed to do *one* thing right last night. I had come to my senses before we actually kissed. That would have been nothing short of total personal ruin. I knew there was no *way* he really wanted to kiss me. He was probably just hoping that a kiss would get me to stop droning on and on about my messed-up life.

True, his eyes had been sort of smoldering when he had been leaning so close . . . but that had most likely been due to fatigue, not desire. I wasn't Jake's type, and I never would be. *Not that I* want *to be,* I assured myself. I found him just as unattractive as he found me!

"Christy, hello, are you listening?" Nicole asked, waving her hand in front of my face.

I blinked. Whoops. I not only didn't know what she had just said—I had no idea what either of them had been talking about for the last five minutes. "Uh, yes, I was listening," I protested. "I think we should look for the mystery guy at all the pizza places nearby."

Jane raised her eyebrows. "Christy, we were asking if you wanted more fries. We were thinking of sharing another order."

Whoops again. "Sorry, guys. I guess I'm sort of preoccupied."

"What were you thinking about?" Nicole asked gently, her big brown eyes filled with sympathy. "Was it your mom?"

"No, not my mom." For once I could say that in all honesty. My mom had been the last thing on my mind as I had gone over the near kiss in my head.

"What, then?" Jane asked. "Do you want to talk about it?"

I bit the inside of my cheek, pondering the question. I knew I could trust Jane and Nicole with anything. They wouldn't go blabbing to anyone about the scene with Jake. And they would probably come up with all sorts of reasons about why I shouldn't feel humiliated.

But what was the point of spilling my guts? Last

night was over, and I wanted to put it behind me. Besides, the Kiss That Never Happened meant zilch to me. I had analyzed the moment enough in my head. I didn't need to do it again in a friends-therapy session.

Besides, I didn't want to give Jane and Nicole the wrong idea. If I told them about last night and the way my body had totally melted when I stared at Jake's lips, they might not believe me when I told them that I couldn't stand the guy.

"I know!" Nicole exclaimed. "You were thinking about Matt."

Matt. Right. The guy I had a huge crush on. "Well . . ." I let my voice trail off, allowing my best friends to interpret my response any way they wanted to.

"Were you daydreaming about kissing him?" Jane asked. "Before Max and I started dating, I must have imagined our first kiss a thousand times."

"Are you in love?" Nicole teased. "Does thinking about Matt make your heart go pitter-pat?"

I rolled my eyes. "No comment," I informed them. "I'll just let you two use your fertile imaginations to fill in the blanks."

"I wonder what it would be like to kiss the mystery man," Nicole mused. "Not that I'll ever have the chance to find out . . ."

As Nicole launched back into a discussion about how to find the guy from Claire's Boutique, I breathed a small sigh of relief. I loved my friends, but there were some things better left unsaid. Anyway, as soon as Jake and I got this prom date behind us, I could quit worrying about him. And as far as I was concerned, that couldn't be soon enough.

"Are you sure you're up for this?" I asked my mother on Friday afternoon. "Because if you're tired, we don't have to stay."

Mom put her arm around my shoulders and gave me her patented squeeze. "I'm fine, honey. Really. I took a long nap before you got home from school, and I woke up feeling quite refreshed."

The prom was tomorrow, and Mom had surprised me when I got home from school by telling me that she had made an appointment for me to get my hair cut and highlighted by a woman at Bijin, the best salon in town. And she had insisted on coming with me.

This was the first time in almost two months that we had been out, just the two of us. I was worried about Mom, but I was also walking on air. It felt great to be doing such a typical mother–daughter activity together.

I returned her squeeze, just like I always did. "Okay. If you're sure."

As we walked into the salon, I saw Mom's eyes shine. Before her hair had started to fall out from the chemotherapy, she had prided herself on what she called "creative expression through hair." Mom never dyed her hair blue or purple, but she had been a blonde, a brunette, and a redhead at various points during my childhood. Her theory was that change on the *outside* fostered growth on the *inside*. I had rebelled by maintaining the same hairstyle since third grade.

"Good afternoon, Mary Ann," my mother greeted her hairstylist enthusiastically. "Christy has finally agreed to go under the scissors—for more than the biannual trim she usually consents to."

Mary Ann grinned. "I've been wanting to get at that head of hair for a decade," she proclaimed. "Christy, this is going to be the first day of the rest of your life."

I resisted the urge to roll my eyes. I thought the two of them were making a little much of a simple haircut and highlight, but I wasn't going to argue. Whatever made Mom happy made *me* happy.

"I'm in your hands, Mary Ann," I proclaimed. "You have complete power over my hair." I smiled. "But please, be gentle."

Fifteen minutes and one shampoo, condition, and head massage later, I was sitting in Mary Ann's chair with a giant smock covering most of my body. Mom was several feet away, sitting across from her favorite manicurist, Eula.

"I feel ten years and five chemo treatments younger," Mom declared. "I should have been getting weekly manicures for the last eighteen months."

"I feel nervous," I admitted. I looked up at Mary Ann. "You're not going to give me a Mohawk or anything, are you?"

121

"I promise that you're going to have the best hair at the prom tomorrow night," Mary Ann assured me. "Trust me."

"So Mom told you about the prom?" I asked.

I wasn't surprised. She had been talking about it all week. The dress, the hair, the makeup, the shoes. I had never realized that going to a dance involved so many accessories.

"Your date sounds like a real hottie," Mary Ann commented as she started to paint sections of my hair with some gooey, bad-smelling concoction.

"Jake is adorable," Mom chimed in. "And he's one of the nicest young men I've ever met."

Usually my mom's judgment about people was right on. But she had a blind spot when it came to Jake Saunders. For some crazy reason, she thought the boy walked on water.

"What about you, Christy?" Mary Ann asked. "Do you think Jake is *adorable*?"

"I'm glad he asked me to the prom," I answered truthfully. I *was* glad. The fact that I was dreading it didn't preclude me from being happy that he had asked me. For my mother's sake.

"I'd like hot pink nail polish," Mom told Eula as the manicurist pulled her hands out of two small tubs of soapy water. "You only live once—I might as well let my presence be known."

"Mom, enough jokes," I called. It was nice that my mom still had her sense of humor intact, but I couldn't laugh along with her cancer jokes. They made me sad.

122

"I'm sorry, honey," she replied. "It's just so good to be out of the house that I'm feeling a little giddy."

"That's okay." I was a horrible daughter. How could I deny my own mother even a second of pleasure? She had the right to say whatever she wanted—I just wished it didn't have such a disturbing ring of truth.

Mary Ann gave me a pat on the shoulder. "Your mom is one of the strongest women I know," she said softly. "She'll get through this."

I hoped Mary Ann was right. But deep down, I knew that she wasn't. Still, now wasn't the time to dwell on matters over which I had no control. Instead I would focus on the light in my mother's eyes and thank God that we had this afternoon at the hairdresser's together.

Every minute was precious, and I didn't intend to forget it. Besides, if Mom could still enjoy life to the fullest, then so could I.

I smiled at Mary Ann in the huge mirror that faced the chair. "Don't hold back on that coloring goo," I instructed her. "Let's go for it!"

That's what Mom and I were doing. We were going for it, right here, right now, in a place where women had sought comfort since the dawn of time. The beauty parlor.

"You know, I think I'm going to get a pedicure too," Mom announced. "Let's throw caution to the wind."

I glanced at my mother. She was starting to look tired, but the light was still in her eyes. And as long as that light was there, she was the person I had always known and loved. Cancer couldn't change that.

"You know what?" I said to my mother, who was waving her left hand in the air to make the polish dry faster.

"What, sweetie?" she asked.

"This is one of the best days of my life." And it was true. I just hoped that the *worst* day in my life was still years and years away.

Thirteen

Christy

I ALMOST DIDN'T recognize myself as I stared into the mirror on Saturday evening. The girl I was looking at was *me*—but a brighter, smoother, more glamorous version. I turned my head from side to side, checking out my new haircut for the tenth time in the last hour and a half.

Mary Ann is a genius, I thought. She belonged in the hairdresser Hall of Fame. I hadn't thought there was anything wrong with my hair before Friday afternoon—it had been brown and straight and went halfway down my back. I wasn't the type of person who tortured herself with curling irons and hair spray. My idea of a good haircut was one that required, like, *no* maintenance.

Now my hair fell just below my shoulders, and Mary Ann had layered it around my face to give it shape and movement. Best of all, she had added golden highlights that made my hair shine and brought out the golden flecks in my hazel eyes.

But it wasn't just my hair that looked different. Earlier Mom had come into my room and done my makeup herself. She had gone all out, using powder, blush, lip liner, and lipstick. But the pièces de résistance were my eyes. Mom had coated the lids in a warm shade of dark gold, then used a charcoal liner. When she had finally brushed black mascara onto the lashes, my eyes had popped out like never before. The overall look was natural but, well, stunning—if I did say so myself.

"Let's hope I have a chance to show it off," I said to myself as I pulled my prom dress off its hanger.

For the last few days there had been a nagging worry at the back of my mind that Jake wasn't going to show up for our prom date. True, he had promised. But that had been before that awful night at his house. Since our conversation on Monday we had barely spoken. In fact, I had gone completely out of my way to avoid him. I hadn't even seen the guy since Thursday morning.

I slipped into the dress, then pulled up the long side zipper. Finally I stepped into the high-heeled strappy sandals I had bought for the occasion. Okay. One last look and then it was countdown time.

Once again I stared at myself in the mirror. The dress I had chosen was simple but elegant. It was strapless, made of deep rose silk, and fell almost to the floor. No ruffles, spangles, or beads for me. But

126

there *was* still something missing. I picked up the small pearl earrings my mother had worn on her prom night and carefully put them on. It was the only jewelry I wanted to wear.

Somehow the earrings made the evening seem real. This was *prom* night. It was the event that teenagers built up in their minds for years—a rite of passage in the journey toward adulthood. If Matt were going to be my date tonight, I would probably be laughing giddily as I stashed an extra lipstick in my evening bag. I would be checking my breath five times, making sure I was prepared for our first kiss on the dance floor.

But Matt wasn't my date. Neither was Zach or Joe or Steven. My date was Jake. And all I felt anticipating his arrival (I hoped) at the door was a vague sense of nausea and a major case of nerves. The most romantic night of my life was going to resemble a train wreck.

"Voilà!" I announced as I walked into the living room, where my parents were awaiting my big entrance.

My mom was lying on the couch, covered by a shawl. She had been feeling basically rotten all day, but she had insisted on both doing my makeup and being downstairs when Jake arrived. Now that I saw her face, I was happy that I hadn't put up a fight, trying to keep her in bed.

"Christy, there's only one word to describe you," Mom gushed. "Beautiful!" She held out her hand for me to take. "And that's on the outside *and* the inside."

My dad reached out and took her other hand. "You look just like Rose," he said softly. "I feel like I'm peering into the past."

"Thanks," I told them. "I have to admit, this is the closest I've ever felt to a fairy princess."

"Honey, this is going to be such a magical night. I want you to forget about *all* of your worries and just enjoy it." She kissed my hand. "You deserve to have a wonderful time."

"I will," I promised her.

I didn't care about the dance. Not really. *This* was the moment I had been waiting for. No matter how the rest of the night progressed, I was declaring the evening a success. The look in Mom's eyes was all of the "wonderful" I needed.

As long as Jake shows up, I added silently. The date himself was as important to Mom as the dress, the earrings, and the vintage handbag.

Dad glanced at his watch. "Jake should be here any second," he commented. "I'll get the camera ready."

He got up and left the room in search of the camera. Once he was gone, I tapped my foot nervously, praying that Jake wasn't going to ditch me at the last minute. *He wouldn't do that,* I told myself. *His mom wouldn't let him even if he wanted to.*

Then again, Jake was stubborn. If he had decided that he couldn't stand spending another minute with me and my tears, nobody was going to change his mind.

"Sweetie, is something wrong?" Mom asked. "You seem anxious."

I stopped tapping. "No, I, uh, was just wondering whether or not Jake is going to like my dress," I lied.

"He will, Christy." Mom pulled the shawl more tightly around her shoulders and let her eyes drift shut. "I'm just going to shut my eyes for a minute before he gets here."

I bit my lip as I watched my mother. She was weaker. I was sure of it. This wasn't just one of her "bad" days. She was losing strength day by day.

In the hallway the doorbell sounded. "He's here!" Dad called, walking back into the living room.

Thank goodness, I thought. Jake had come through.

Mom's eyes opened. "Get the door, honey. Dad and I will wait in here."

I took a deep breath and walked to the door. *Here we go,* I thought. *The moment of truth.*

"Hi, Christy." Jake's voice was friendly but distant. Sort of like he was greeting his second cousin twice removed who he'd only met once before.

I wasn't prepared for my physical reaction to Jake in a tuxedo. He looked amazing. He had even gotten a haircut. I stood there, trying to think of something to say.

"Nice to see you, Jake," he said. "Why, thank you. Nice to see you too, Christy."

"Oh, s–sorry," I stammered. "Nice to see you, Jake."

"You changed your hair." He said it as if I had broken some cardinal rule of prom going.

"What? You hate it?" I asked, feeling self-conscious.

He shook his head. "No, I, uh, it looks, uh, pretty."

I stood back to let him inside, and when he moved away from the door, I saw a white stretch limo waiting at the curb. "Whoa. Nice ride," I commented. "What happened to Ramona?"

He grinned. "She's taking the night off."

"Thanks for being here, Jake," I told him, mustering all of my dignity. "And thank you for all of the nice touches. It'll mean a lot to my mom."

Jake smiled. "Hey, when I take a girl to the prom, I take her to the *prom.*"

"Don't keep us in suspense," my mother called from the living room. "Get in here, you two."

Jake took my hand and pulled me into the living room. "Hey, Mr. and Mrs. Redmond," he greeted them. "I have come to whisk your beautiful daughter to the winter wonderland we're promised the gym has been transformed into."

"Jake, you look incredibly handsome," Mom declared. "I'll be sure to give your mom copies of the dozen pictures we're going to take."

"Please don't," Jake asked. "She'll turn them into T-shirts and hand them out at the next family reunion."

Mom laughed. "You see, Christy?" she said. "I'm not the only overzealous mother in this neighborhood."

In that second all of the anger and resentment I had been feeling toward Jake since the other night seemed to melt away. He had made my mom laugh. And he was here. With a limo. And compliments.

130

And a gorgeous corsage that he was about to pin to my waist. I couldn't remember the last time I had felt so grateful to another human being.

"Stand by the fireplace while you do the corsage," Mom instructed. "It'll be a great photo."

I felt like a complete idiot as Jake and I posed in front of the fireplace. But I couldn't help grinning when my dad yelled, "Cheese." Mom was acting like she was sixteen years old, ordering us into poses and cracking one corny joke after another.

There was the picture of him pinning on the corsage. The picture of me pinning on *his* boutonniere. The picture of us with our arms around each other, facing the camera. The picture of us with our arms around each other, looking at each other. The list went on and on until the roll was finished.

"Have a wonderful time," Mom said when she finally felt satisfied with her photo-album material. "And *don't* think about us." *Translation: Don't think about* me, I thought.

"I'll have her back by dawn," Jake promised as we headed out the door. "Don't wait up!"

As we walked toward the limo, my dad waving in the doorway, I knew what I had to do. I had to apologize to Jake for the way I had blown him off in the library. Maybe we weren't best friends, but he deserved my respect at the very least. There weren't that many guys in the world who would be willing to give up their own prom night just to make their mom's friend happy. He was one in a million.

★　　★　　★

131

Once we were alone in the back of the limo, my heart started to pound. *It's not because we're alone,* I told myself. *It's because I know what I have to do.*

"I'm sorry for being such a jerk," I blurted out. "You're not a tottering, elf-skinned hedge-pig."

Jake laughed. "Christy, I think that's the biggest compliment you've ever given me." He paused. "But truthfully, I'm just glad you're speaking to me again. I was worried we were going to spend the entire evening in icy silence."

"I've been so confused lately," I confessed. "One minute I'm happy, the next I'm crying." I sighed.

He laughed. "We're seventeen," he pointed out. "We're supposed to be confused."

"So, we're friends, such as it is?" I asked, holding out my hand.

"Friends—such as it is." Jake shook my hand firmly as the driver pulled the limousine into the Union High parking lot.

I looked out the window and saw none other than Wendy Schultz walking into the prom with her date. I opened my mouth to make a snappy comment, then abruptly shut it.

The atmosphere between Jake and me had started to thaw. I didn't want to do anything to change that. Not now, after he had been so understanding about my wacky behavior.

Maybe for one night we can have a truce, I thought. *Maybe we can even have some fun.*

132

Fourteen

Jake

ONCE WE GOT inside the dance, Christy started to ooh and aah over the decorations. And they were pretty impressive. The Union High gymnasium had been transformed, as promised, into a veritable winter wonderland.

But I barely registered the hundreds of twinkling lights or the tiny tables or even the huge disco ball hanging over the center of the dance floor. My gaze was firmly fixed on Christy, as it had been since the moment she opened the door tonight.

Two words, one girl: *absolutely fabulous.* When Christy had greeted me at the door, I felt like I had been punched in the stomach. I had seen her thousands of times in my life. I had even been aware of her subtle beauty for what seemed like forever. But tonight I felt like I was seeing Christy for the first time.

The way her hair brushed lightly against her shoulders made my fingers itch to reach out and touch her smooth, ivory skin. And when I looked into the depths of her hazel eyes, I felt like I was tumbling headfirst into a pool of lava. *It's just the dress,* I told myself. *You're reacting to a girl in a beautiful, sophisticated, pink . . . creation.*

Except that it wasn't the dress. Christy had been infiltrating my thoughts for weeks. Thanks to her, I hadn't even been in the right frame of mind to go on an actual date with a *normal* girl since I asked her to the prom. That wasn't like me. In fact, it was the *opposite* of me.

When Christy had reached out to shake my hand in the back of the limo, I had felt like I'd been zapped with electricity. Never had a friendly handshake made such an impression. I had been instantly beamed back in time to that night on the sofa in my bedroom. I had been right back at that near kiss.

I knew with one hundred percent of my intellectual capability that Christy and I could never be a couple. We agreed on nothing, and we had raised bickering to the level of high art. It was guaranteed that an extended conversation with Christy was going to reduce me to a blithering, stuttering fool.

That's what my *head* told me. But when I spotted Matt Fowler on the other side of the gym, doing his lame imitation of Ricky Martin, my heart told me something else. I couldn't bear the idea of watching Christy flirt with that stupid guy.

Matt had the personality of a bad used-car salesman.

Sure, he was good-looking. But so what? Ted Bundy had been a charming guy, and he turned out to be a serial killer. Okay, maybe Matt wasn't felon material.

Nonetheless, he wasn't worthy of someone like Christy. Yes, she had faults too numerous to name. But she also had fire and strength and intelligence and wit and an inner light that made her shine even in the worst of times. It was my *duty* to keep her from making the mistake of falling for that guy. As an old friend, it was the least I could do.

"Why don't we dance?" I suggested as Christy stood gazing around the already crowded prom.

"We don't have to, Jake," she responded. "I appreciate the offer, but a deal is a deal. Now that we're here, you're officially off the hook."

I had to play this carefully. "I really think we should hit the dance floor for a couple of numbers," I insisted. "That way you can tell your mom all about it when you get home."

I wasn't being *totally* manipulative. I really did think that Rose would badger Christy for all of the details about her prom experience.

Christy nodded. "You're right," she agreed finally. "And I promise I won't step on your toes unless I absolutely can't help it."

"Deal." I clasped her hand and led her toward the center of the dance floor.

Holding Christy's hand, my palms felt as sweaty as they had the fateful night of our first and only date. Thankfully, I had matured enough to realize that the way to deal with nerves was *not* to insult my date and proceed to make a complete idiot of myself. Instead I would simply take the next opportunity to surreptitiously wipe my palms on my tux pants.

I took Christy in my arms as the band struck up a rendition of "Let's Fall in Love." I half expected her to cringe as I placed my hands on her waist, but she didn't. She put one hand on my shoulder, the other on my waist, and began to move to the music.

"This is nice," Christy commented. "I haven't danced since I went to homecoming with Michael Farley my sophomore year."

Ugh. Michael Farley. Two years above us, the guy had been a walking ego. But I kept my mouth shut. I wasn't about to incur Christy's wrath at this particular juncture by issuing an ill-conceived opinion of her ex-flame.

"Uh-huh . . . ," I answered in a noncommittal voice.

Christy laughed softly. "That guy was the biggest loser. He kept telling me that if I was lucky, he would 'give me something to write about in my diary.'" She quirked an eyebrow. "Lucky for me, I didn't *have* a diary."

"Sounds like a gem." I wasn't going to fall into this trap. I knew girls. They could insult past dates, but far be it from anyone else to chime in on the conversation.

"Anyway, you're a much better dancer than he was," Christy assured me. She paused. "Is it my imagination, or am I sort of talking to myself here?"

"I don't know what you mean." I twirled her around, hoping the touch of finesse would impress her.

"I mentioned Michael Farley, who I *know* you hate, and you didn't even react." She looked up at me, her eyes sparkling. "Is the great Jake Saunders at a loss for words for the first time in his life?"

"I, uh . . ." I wanted to say something witty. But I couldn't. I had been struck completely dumb by the nearness of Christy's lips to mine. "I don't even remember who he is," I said finally. "Although I do have a vague image of a giant pumpkin attached to a hormonally challenged body."

Christy grinned. "Now, that's the Jake I know and love." She gasped. "I mean, the Jake I *know*. The love part was just a figure of speech."

"Right. Of course." We needed more dancing and less talking. I was getting dumber by the second.

Why? Because this tiny, traitorous part of myself had positively come alive when the word *love* had escaped (and I mean that literally) Christy's mouth. What did it mean?

"If you're quiet because you're concentrating on locating Wendy, she's on the other side of the dance floor," Christy informed me.

Wendy who? I thought. I hadn't thought of her once since we had arrived at the prom. In fact, I hadn't exchanged more than a few pleasantries with Wendy Schultz since that night in my room. That night. That night. That night. Why couldn't I get it off my mind?

"I'll catch up with her later," I told Christy. "I

was actually thinking about something else. I was, um, wondering if you were getting thirsty."

"Are you?" Christy asked.

No! I wanted to scream. *I'm not hungry or thirsty or thinking about Wendy Schultz.* I just wanted to pull Christy close and spend the rest of the night barely moving on the dance floor. I wanted to inhale her perfume and rub my cheek against hers and whisper into her ear.

"I'm fine," I told her. "I really like this song."

So what if I had no idea *what* song the band had just started to play? It was slow; it was romantic; it was good enough for me.

"Do you want to go find Jane and Nicole?" I asked. "They're probably here by now."

I knew how much girls liked to confer at events like these. They could spend hours discussing dresses, makeup, and fashion faux pas. As much as I wanted to keep dancing, I wasn't going to hold Christy here against her will. It wasn't my style.

"I'll find them later. I, uh, really like this song too." She seemed to drop the idea of leaving the dance floor in search of a cup of sticky, overly sweet punch or someone better to talk to. Christy's eyes were closed as she swayed back and forth.

As I studied her sweet, serene face, the truth hit me. The tenderness I was feeling toward Christy had nothing to do with her mother's illness. And it had nothing to do with the fact that we had known each other forever. The truth didn't even have anything to do with her beautiful dress or the intoxicating scent of her hair.

Christy had gotten under my skin. I was falling all over again for this frustrating, somewhat crazy girl. I had been falling for her for a long time, but I hadn't let myself admit it. The idea was too overwhelming, too scary.

It's hopeless, I told myself. Christy and I were a match made in . . . I didn't know where. All I knew was that every time we got together, catastrophe seemed to ensue. *But we're getting along okay right now,* I argued with myself.

Maybe Christy and I had experienced a few rough years. But did that mean we were destined to snipe at each other every time our paths crossed? Again my head answered that question one way, my heart another.

I pulled Christy closer, testing the waters. She didn't protest. She sort of melted into my embrace as if being in such close proximity to my body was the most natural thing in the world.

I rested my head against hers and closed my eyes. Maybe there was hope for the two of us after all. . . .

Fifteen

Christy

"HAVE ANOTHER SUGAR cookie," Jake offered. "It's on me."

I made a gagging motion. "I can't believe I choked *one* of those down. There's no way I'm going to try for two."

Jake grinned, snapping the hard-as-a-rock sugar cookie in half. "This cookie could have been used as one of a caveman's first tools," he commented, depositing the cookie onto a tiny paper plate.

I raised my glass of punch. "What about this stuff? It tastes like strawberry-flavored cough syrup."

He put his own cup to his mouth and downed the contents in one huge gulp. "Aaah . . . refreshing!"

"Yuck!" I giggled. Jake's face was slightly contorted,

but he was smiling as if he had just downed a delicious cup of hot chocolate.

"So, what do you say?" he asked. "Are you ready to head back out to the dance floor? I heard a rumor that the band is going to play the hokey-pokey next."

"Let's do it."

It wasn't until Jake and I were wending our way through the dancing couples that I realized how bizarre it was that we were voluntarily going back to the floor for another round of dancing together.

I had been so busy laughing and talking with Jake that I hadn't even thought about the fact that we'd practically had a written contract to stay away from each other once we arrived at the prom. It had seemed natural for us to stick together.

As I continued to follow Jake through the crowd, I thought about what Jane had said. We had grabbed a couple of minutes for girl talk when Jake and Max had been standing in line for the dreaded punch together.

"You and Jake make such an amazing couple," Jane had exclaimed. "I don't know why I never saw that before."

I hadn't known how to respond to Jane's comment. It had come out of absolutely nowhere and landed like a slap on the face. Jake and me? An amazing couple? The notion was ludicrous, absurd, and outlandish—all rolled up into one.

And yet . . . I hadn't come out and said that to her. I had just stood there stuttering until, mercifully, the guys had shown up with our glasses of punch. But with that one sentence my entire night had taken a turn. The power of suggestion was an incredible phenomenon. I simply couldn't look at Jake through the same lens I had been using for the past five years.

"You don't mind if I pull out my *Saturday Night Fever* moves, do you?" Jake asked. "I saw it on cable the other night, and I've been itching to disco ever since."

We had reached the center of the dance floor, and Jake was jumping up and down as if he were a runner trying to limber up.

"Feel free. Just make sure to avoid eye contact with me," I teased him. "I don't want to be seen on the floor with a guy who wishes he were in a white suit and platform shoes."

"All right, all right," he conceded. "I'll save the disco moves for the privacy of my own home."

Jake put his arms around me, and I experienced the same melting sensation that I had earlier in the evening when he had pulled me close. By the time we left the floor in search of refreshment, I felt like a piece of taffy that had been left in the backseat of a car on an August afternoon.

The prom was turning out to be more fun than I ever could have imagined. Correction. *Jake* was turning out to be more fun than I could have imagined. It was like I had stepped into some alternate universe in which Jake and I had never had that terrible date that ended our friendship.

I liked dancing with him. He was graceful—but

not a show-off. And he knew just how to hold me. In fact, I liked dancing with Jake *too much*. It was one thing to feel like we were in the process of re-discovering our lost friendship. But I found myself wishing he would hold me tighter.

I'm attracted to him, I admitted to myself. This wasn't like the other night on his sofa. I couldn't blame my feelings on being upset. I wasn't in tears now, searching for any human connection I could find. This was pure physical attraction.

"Get ready for the dip!" Jake exclaimed. "We're really going to go for it this time."

I braced myself. Jake was a good dancer, but he had dropped me on the floor the last time we had attempted this move. Of course, I hadn't helped matters by losing my footing when my heel caught on the hem of my dress.

"Ready and waiting, Fred," I told him.

Clasping his hand, I took a few steps back. Then I twirled counterclockwise until our bodies collided. Immediately Jake put his other arm around my waist and dipped me so low to the ground that my hair brushed the floor.

From my upside-down position I spotted Matt, dancing several couples away. Matt! I had completely forgotten about him.

"Yes!" Jake yelled, pulling me upright. "The judges would have to give us a ten for that dip—if there were any." He grinned. "Nice job, Ginger."

I laughed. "Fred, without you, I'm two left feet."

As I drifted back into Jake's arms, I knew that it

wasn't the blood that had rushed to my head that was making me dizzy. It was Jake.

It was crazy, but the only place I wanted to be right now was right here with *him*. I had zero interest in going over and saying hi to Matt. I had even avoided making eye contact with him a couple of times already. I was afraid that he was going to remind me of my promise to save him a dance.

You're an idiot, I told myself. At this very moment Jake was probably plotting how to get rid of me so that he could flirt his way through every available girl in the room. He and Wendy Schultz most likely had some synchronized plan that involved the two of them meeting in an abandoned broom closet for a major make-out session.

"Just let me know when you're ready to try the tango," Jake whispered in my ear. "Thanks to my mother, I've had to watch Al Pacino tango in *Scent of a Woman* three times."

Jake is having fun too, I realized. A guy who wasn't enjoying himself didn't crack jokes and goof around. And I couldn't help but notice that Jake hadn't even glanced in Wendy's direction. Or anyone else's, for that matter. He had been the perfect date since he arrived at my doorstep.

The music slowed, and Jake pulled me closer. "Everybody else is dancing cheek to cheek," he pointed out. "We, uh, might as well go with the flow."

"Yeah, sure," I agreed breezily. But inside, my heart was fluttering and my stomach had dropped to my feet.

I was overwhelmed—with emotions and desire and, strangely, fear. I had never felt this way before. At least, not since seventh grade, when I had spent every waking moment thinking about . . . Jake.

Jake's arms tightened around my waist. We were so close that I could feel his heart beating. Was this real? Was Jake experiencing the same flurry of emotions that I was?

Or is he just being nice to me because he feels sorry for me? I wondered. Was it possible that Jake was trying to make me feel good because he knew that I was going through the worst time of my life? I had thought so the night that Jake and I had almost kissed. I had been sure of it. The pity kiss.

But my heart wasn't letting me believe that Jake was only hanging out with me because of his loyalty to my mother. I had seen the sparkle in his eyes, and I had heard his laughter. Jake hadn't *had* to hold me so close. And he couldn't make his heart beat that way—not if he weren't genuinely feeling *something*.

But this didn't make any sense. This wasn't the way Jake and I related. We were combative and surly and sarcastic.

"I need to go to the ladies' room," I said suddenly, pushing away from him. "I'll be back in a minute."

I needed space. And time to think. I had to sort out these confusing feelings before I started to fall for Jake in a big way. *Except I'm afraid it's too late for that,* I thought. *I think I've already fallen.*

★   ★   ★

I'll think about Jake in a minute, I decided once I was in the girls' locker room. First I wanted to call home and check on Mom.

Yes, she had told me to have a great time and not give her a second thought. But that was like telling me not to breathe. She had been happy this evening, but she had also been in pain. I wouldn't be able to think with absolute clarity until I knew she was okay.

I took thirty-five cents out of my evening bag and dropped it into the pay phone that stood in the corner of the locker room. As I dialed our family's phone number, I said a silent prayer of hope. Hope that Mom wasn't in any pain. Hope that she was feeling great. Hope that her cancer had miraculously disappeared while Jake and I had been dancing and drinking fruit punch.

"Hello?" The voice that answered the phone didn't belong to either of my parents. It was Jake's mom.

Why is she there? I wondered. Nobody had mentioned that she was coming by tonight. Jake had told me that his parents had rented a movie and were planning to make homemade pizza.

"Hi, Mrs. Saunders," I said, my heart lurching. "It's Christy. I wanted to check in and see how Mom was doing."

"Christy, honey. Hi."

I felt like I was going to throw up. Molly never called me "honey." "How is she?" I asked again. "Tell me."

There was a pause. "Your dad took her to the

hospital," she said finally. "I came over so that I could tell you when you got home."

"Oh no," I whispered. "Please, no."

"They wanted you to enjoy the prom," Mrs. Saunders continued. "There's nothing you can do at the hospital."

"This isn't happening," I said, more to myself than to Molly. "Is it . . . what's going on, exactly?" I asked breathlessly.

"I don't know, Christy," she responded, her voice filled with sadness. "But you might want to . . ."

I didn't hear the rest of what she said. I hung up the phone and sprinted out of the locker room. I had to get to the hospital. Now! My mother could be dying at this very moment, and I wasn't there.

I pushed my way through the gym, tears streaming down my face. I didn't stop to talk to Jake. I didn't stop to talk to anyone. There was no time for questions or hugs or sympathetic gestures. I just wanted to get out of there quickly as I possibly could.

Finally I burst through the gymnasium door. I slipped out of my sandals as I scanned the parking lot, searching for the driver who had brought Jake and me to the prom.

Suddenly I felt a hand on my arm. "Christy?" a soft voice asked.

I turned my head and found myself looking at Nicole's mystery man. She had finally located him, and they were here at the prom together. I had seen them several times, but they hadn't come over to say hello yet. So how did he know my name?

He was talking to me, but I couldn't really hear what he was saying. I just knew that I saw understanding in his dark brown eyes. Not just sympathy . . . but real understanding.

How could he know anything about my mom? Before I had a chance to even ask him, he explained. His name was Justin, and his own mother had died of cancer last year. He'd seen me in the cancer ward last year. I hadn't remembered Justin until now. Maybe I hadn't wanted to.

I told him that my mom had gotten worse. "Please don't tell anyone that you saw me," I said finally. "I'm not ready to talk about this."

"I won't tell the others," he told me, handing me his prom ticket with a phone number written on it. "Promise that you'll call me if you ever want to talk. I really do know what you're going through."

I nodded and squeezed his hand, vaguely thinking that Nicole had chosen a great stranger as her prom date. I was looking wildly around for the driver of the limo that Jake had rented. At last I spotted him. He was standing next to the limousine. I hiked up my dress and raced to his side.

"I need to get to Memorial Hospital right way," I told him. "It's an emergency."

"Of course," he responded.

I dove into the back of the limo as the driver slid into the driver's seat and gunned the engine. "We'll be there in ten minutes," he assured me.

I closed my eyes. *I'm on my way, Mom,* I told her silently. *Just hang on until I get there.*

Sixteen

Jake

AFTER ABOUT FIVE seconds of standing alone on the dance floor, I realized that it wasn't a place where I wanted to be solo. It doesn't take long for a guy dancing by himself to start looking like a major geek. But I didn't want to find another partner (like Wendy, who had been glancing my way all night) either. I wanted to dance with Christy. Period.

Finally I maneuvered my way off the dance floor, keeping my eye out for Christy as I headed toward the edge of the crowd. Now I stood several yards from the door to the girls' locker room, where I would be sure to spot her the moment she walked out of the bathroom.

I tapped my foot and glanced at my watch. She had been gone almost fifteen minutes. Girls! Once they all congregated in the women's room, they could spend up to an hour gabbing about who knew what.

But I was getting impatient. And from the other side of the gymnasium I could see Wendy slowly making her way in my direction. I needed to find Christy—ASAP.

"Hey, Jenny, was Christy Redmond in there?" I asked as Jenny Leland walked out of the locker room.

Jenny shook her head. "Nope. Sorry."

Great. She had left the locker room. Now what? I scanned the dance floor, searching for Christy's pink dress. But I didn't see her. Suddenly I had a horrible thought. What if Christy had ditched me so she could hang out with Matt Fowler?

It's no big deal, I told myself. It was a free country. Christy could do whatever she wanted. But it *was* a big deal. I didn't *want* Christy to be off somewhere with Matt. I wanted her to be by my side or, more accurately, in my arms.

I started to walk around the perimeter of the gymnasium, searching for Christy. My heart dropped when I saw none other than Matt Fowler standing in a corner. His back was to me, and he appeared to be kissing someone. Christy!

Then I saw a brief flash of mint green. *Encouraging,* I thought. I walked closer to Matt and craned my neck so that I could see who he was kissing. Phew. It was Sandra Donell, his date.

So Christy wasn't with Matt. I continued my

journey around the perimeter of the dance, keeping my eyes peeled for that beautiful pink dress, that shiny head of dark hair. I didn't see Nicole or her date. I *did* see Jane and Max, but they seemed oblivious to the rest of the world—as they had been for the majority of the evening.

I reached my original post near the girls' locker room, and still I hadn't even glimpsed Christy. *Maybe she went outside,* I thought. It was pretty hot in here—I wouldn't mind getting a little fresh air myself.

It was the only explanation. I picked up my pace and more or less jogged to the entrance of the gymnasium. Outside, I inhaled the fresh, sweet air and scanned the parking lot for Christy.

Plenty of people were out there, but none of them was wearing a pink dress. As I walked among the cars and limousines that were parked outside, I noticed that Christy wasn't the only person missing. I didn't see our driver, Ted, anywhere.

I approached a couple of limo drivers who were hanging out next to one of their vehicles. "Hey, have you seen a guy named Ted?" I asked. "Long hair, goatee, black cap?"

One of the guys nodded. "Yeah, Ted. He was here a while ago. But he took off with some girl."

My stomach felt like it had just been twisted into a giant pretzel. "Was she wearing a pink dress?" I asked.

The guy nodded. "Yeah. And she was *hot.*" He grinned. "Sorry, guy. Looks like you lost your date."

I felt like punching him. Instead I turned and headed back to the prom. This was nuts! One second everything was great. The next second Christy had abandoned me in the middle of the dance floor and hijacked our limo.

Why would she do that? I asked myself. Nobody, not even Christy, would do something so blatantly rude. Not unless there was a logical explanation.

Suddenly I stopped in my tracks. Christy *wouldn't* have left the prom without a good reason. I was sure of it. If nothing else, she wouldn't want to explain to her mom why she was home early.

Mrs. Redmond. I walked to a pay phone outside the gymnasium, hoping against hope that the pit in my stomach was simply the result of too many sugar cookies. *Please let me be wrong,* I prayed as I fished thirty-five cents out of the pocket of my tux pants.

My dad answered the phone on the first ring. When I heard his voice, the pit in my stomach transformed itself into a stabbing knife.

"Dad, is everything okay?" I asked. "I'm at the prom, but Christy disappeared. . . ."

"It's Rose," Dad said, his voice heavy and sad. "She went to the hospital about an hour ago. Christy called home, and Mom gave her the news. I guess she didn't want to take the time to tell you what was going on." He paused. "Mom said she hung up the phone before your mother had even finished speaking."

"I need to go to the hospital," I announced. "I need to be there for Christy. But the limo is gone. . . ."

"We were going to head over to Memorial too," Dad said. "Wait outside, and we'll pick you up in ten minutes."

"Thanks." I hung up the phone, feeling like a total jerk.

I shouldn't have thought for one second that Christy was off with Matt or had decided to strand me at the dance. She wasn't that kind of person.

Now I was going to be there for her. I wanted to be by Christy's side—even if she didn't want me to be.

It was after midnight, and so far I hadn't seen Christy. The waiting room at Memorial Hospital was a depressing place: plastic chairs, two vending machines, that antiseptic smell. I had flipped through a dozen issues of *Time* magazine, but none of the articles held my attention.

I had learned from my parents that Mrs. Redmond's condition had worsened shortly after Christy and I had left for the prom. She had taken an extra pain pill, but it had done no good. Finally Mr. Redmond had called my parents and told them that he was taking Rose to the emergency room. Mom had gone to the house to wait for Christy so she could give her the news.

My mom and dad sat on the chairs opposite me. Every once in a while one of them would doze off. Then they would wake up with a start and ask if there had been any word. Each time the answer was no.

Finally I glimpsed Christy coming down the hallway. I sat up straight in my chair and braced myself for bad news. But her face was a complete blank, almost as if she were suffering from shock.

"Christy!" Mom exclaimed as soon as she saw her. "How is she?"

"She's stable—for now." Christy's voice held a note of resignation that broke my heart. "And they've given her a major dose of pain medication. She's asleep."

Mom stood up and folded Christy into her arms, rocking her back and forth. "If there's *anything* we can do, you just say the word."

My mother sounded strong now, in front of Christy, but she had been crying on and off for the past two hours. She had been holding my father's hand so tightly that her knuckles turned white.

"Thank you, Molly." Christy disentangled herself and brushed a tear from her cheek. "But all we can really do now is hope for a miracle."

And then she saw me. "Jake, hey." She saw that I was still in my tuxedo, and she glanced down at herself. She seemed to have forgotten that she was walking around the hospital in a ball gown. "I'm sorry I left like that. . . . I just had to get here as fast as I could."

I shook my head. "Of course. Don't worry about it."

I wanted to say something else. I wanted to tell her how sorry I was, and I wanted to hug her and kiss her and wipe away her tears. But I felt paralyzed.

"Coffee," Christy whispered. "I think I need a cup of black coffee."

"There's a machine around the corner," I told her. "Let's get a cup."

Now that I had a mission, I sprang into action. I jumped out of my seat and rushed to Christy's side.

Then I took her arm and gently guided her to the coffee machine.

Christy sighed and slumped against the wall as I poured her a cup of hot, black coffee. "You don't have to be here," she said quietly. "I appreciate it. But there's nothing anyone can really do right now."

I set the coffee down on top of the machine and turned so that I could look in her eyes. "This is the only place I want to be right now," I told her. "And not just because I care about your mom. I want to be here for *you*."

Another tear slid down Christy's cheek. I reached out and brushed it away, then put my arms around her. She felt so fragile, I wished I could protect her from everything bad in the world.

"Thanks so much, Jake," she whispered. "It means a lot to me to hear you say that."

"I'm going to be here for as long as you need me," I assured her.

She pulled away and took my hands in hers. "You've been an incredible friend, and I'll never forget it."

Again I took her in my arms and hugged her tight. "You'll get through this," I promised. "I know you will."

I wished more than anything that I had some magical power to make all of this go away. But I didn't. No one did. All we could do now was wait . . . and as Christy had said, hope for a miracle.

Seventeen

Christy

ON SUNDAY MORNING I stood by my father's side as Dr. Ziegler came out to speak to us. She had been my mother's doctor since all of this began, and I had come to trust her. She was always sensitive but honest. I knew she would tell us the truth, no matter how painful.

We had been sitting in the small lounge at the end of my mother's hall since they had admitted her to the hospital and moved her from the ER to the oncology ward. Neither of us had suggested leaving. We had simply dozed off in our chairs until sunlight began to stream through the windows.

"How is she?" Dad asked, his voice wavering. "Is Rose any better?"

Dr. Ziegler shook her head. "I'm sorry, Robert. Rose is very weak."

"Is she going to be able to leave the hospital?" I asked. It was the question that would determine everything.

"No, I don't think so, Christy," the doctor answered. "We've done everything we can, and Rose has put up a brave fight. But sometimes these diseases are too powerful to overcome." She paused. "As long as your mother is here, we can make her as comfortable as possible. That just couldn't be done at home. Not at this stage."

"We'll want to be with her twenty-four hours a day," Dad told Dr. Ziegler. "I assume that won't be a problem."

As they continued to speak in hushed tones, I felt my mind leaving my body. I was standing there—still wearing that ridiculous prom dress— but I was watching myself from above. I simply couldn't process this information.

My world was splintering into a million tiny pieces. It was cracking apart, like a precious Ming vase smashing against a tiled floor. The doctor was telling us that it was time to give up the last vestige of hope.

Mom was going to die. Maybe not today. Maybe not tomorrow. But soon. And there was absolutely nothing I could do about it. I couldn't even cry right now. I had to be strong for my dad, and I knew my mom wouldn't want to spend her last days with us being complete basket cases. We had to make every minute count.

I came back into my body and looked at Dr.

160

Ziegler. "Is she awake now?" I asked. "Can I talk to her?"

She nodded. "Rose is awake, and she's quite lucid. I've just had a long talk with her."

So she knew. Mom knew that she was never again going to leave the hospital. A long time ago she had asked us to be straight with her. Dad and I had both promised that we wouldn't hide the truth from her. The doctor had made that same promise, and I had no doubt that she had given Mom the cruel, undeniable facts.

"Can I be alone with her for a few minutes?" I asked my father.

He nodded. "Of course, honey." He put an arm around me. "You go on in. I want to ask the doctor a few more questions anyway."

I stood on my tiptoes and kissed my dad on the cheek. Then I took a deep breath and crossed the short distance to my mother's private hospital room.

Outside the door, I peered through the window and saw Mom sitting up in bed, staring out of the window. She looked contemplative . . . but surprisingly peaceful. I forced myself to smile. I was going to be the first person she saw since she got the news, and I didn't want to be a downer.

I'm here, Mom, I thought. *And I love you.*

"Hi, sweetie," Mom greeted me as soon as I walked into the room. "How are you?"

I walked to her bed and perched beside her so

that I could hold her hand. "I'm fine, Mom." I took her hand in mine. "How are *you?*"

She smiled. "Well, I've been better, honey. But I'm glad you're here."

I choked back tears as I squeezed her hand. "We just talked to the doctor. She told us. . . ."

Mom nodded. "We don't need to think about that right now, sweetie." She paused. "I want to talk about you and Dad and anything under the sun that doesn't have to do with cancer."

"Okay, Mom. Whatever you want."

Suddenly Mom put her hand over mine and sat up a little straighter. She looked right into my eyes. "Christy, we don't have a lot of time left together. Promise me, mother to daughter, that from this second forward you'll tell me *everything* that's in your heart. I don't want to waste this precious time discussing the weather or movies or what medication they're feeding me through this tube stuck in my arm."

"There's so much to say," I whispered. "I don't know where to begin."

She grinned. Only my mother could be attached to tubes and monitors and still manage to smile as if she were sitting down to tea with a couple of friends. I knew already that this was how I would remember her. Smiling. Laughing. Loving.

"Let's start with something simple," she suggested. "First of all, I want to say that I'm sorry you had to leave the prom early. I wanted you to stay and enjoy every second—but I should have known that my loyal, dutiful daughter would call home to check on her sick ol' mom."

"I didn't care about the prom," I told her. "To tell you the truth, I didn't even really want to go."

She looked shocked. "You didn't?" she asked. "But you were so excited. You and Jake had such a wonderful evening planned." She paused. "Why didn't you want to go?"

"It's a long story." I sighed, but I couldn't help smiling a little bit as I thought of Jake. "It's not that I didn't want to go to the prom itself. . . . I just didn't want to go with Jake."

I paused, wondering if I should tell her the whole truth. Then I remembered what she had asked of me, and I took a deep breath. From this moment forward, I was resolved to share everything that was in my heart with my mother. It was the only chance I would have to do so.

"The only reason Jake asked me was because he knew how much it meant to you," I admitted. "And I agreed to be his date for the same reason. We wanted to make you happy."

Mom let go of my hand and took my face in her hands. "Christy, I'm so sorry. I'm touched that you two wanted to please me, but it wasn't necessary."

I smiled. "The weirdest part is that I actually *liked* being his prom date," I told her. "We were dancing together and laughing. . . . I felt like I was in a movie."

"I'm glad, honey." Mom smiled, but her eyes had a faraway look. I guessed that she was remembering her own youth and the times she had spent with my father when they were my age.

"Mom, how did you know that Jake and I might belong together?" I asked. "I mean, up until the last couple of weeks, I couldn't stand the guy!"

"Someday you'll have children of your own," she responded. "And then you'll realize that a mother's intuition is almost always right."

"But I don't know how Jake feels about *me*," I told her. "I mean, I don't even understand my own emotions."

Again my mom smiled. "Christy, growing up is a long, painful process. Maybe Jake is the boy for you, and maybe he isn't." She paused, as if searching for exactly the right words with which to impart her maternal instinct. "The important thing is that you always follow your heart. Don't concern yourself with what other people want or think you should be—and that includes Dad and me."

"But I want you to be *proud* of me," I told her. "That means everything."

Her eyes welled with tears. "Christy, I *am* proud of you. You're a wonderful daughter and a wonderful human being." A lone tear slid down her cheek, but she was still radiating that beautiful, peaceful smile. "All I want is your happiness."

"Thanks, Mom." I leaned down and hugged her tight. Despite her frailty, the warmth of her embrace still had the power to make me believe in myself and in the future.

As we hugged, I thought of the hug Jake had

given me last night when I had gone downstairs to get a cup of coffee and tell the Saunderses about her condition. That hug had also made me feel safe and protected.

Mom had said that all she wanted was my happiness. And I was starting to believe that Jake was a key element to realizing that happiness. But it wasn't something I could contemplate right now.

I was going to focus every ounce of my time and energy on my mother. From this point until . . . the end . . . she was the only person who mattered.

Eighteen

Christy

A WEEK HAD passed since Mom had been admitted to the hospital. I couldn't believe how different this Saturday night was from last weekend. The prom seemed like a distant memory—a haze of twinkling lights, taffeta dresses, and slow, melodic ballads. Now my whole world consisted of doctors, nurses, hospital food, and the constant tests my mother was undergoing in order to have her condition monitored.

I had been to school a few times, but my teachers had been incredibly understanding. Each and every one had told me not to worry about upcoming final exams and term papers. Instead they had arranged to give any necessary assignments to Jane and Nicole, who had come to the hospital every day after school.

Jake had been by at least once a day, entertaining all of us with funny anecdotes about his day in school. And then there was Molly. She had supplied us with an endless number of sumptuous lunches and dinners, both at home and at the hospital.

Home. It seemed almost as far away as the prom. Dad and I had taken turns going to the house to shower and change or catch a few hours of sleep, but neither of us had been able to stay away from Mom longer than was absolutely necessary. Even when she was asleep—which had been most of the time—we had kept a bedside vigil. Neither of us wanted to miss a moment with her.

The days at the hospital had taken on such a familiar routine that I had been lulled into a sense that things had become almost normal again. It had seemed that we would go on like this forever. Mom would be sick, and Dad and I would be there to hold her hand and tell her that we loved her.

But as I looked at Dr. Ziegler's face now, I crashed back to planet Earth. Her eyes told me what I had dreaded hearing for almost two years now. Mom had taken that final turn for the worse. The one that meant the end of her life wasn't only a certainty—it was imminent.

She's been in pain, I told myself. *I don't want her to suffer forever.* But selfishly I *did* want her to keep suffering if it meant that I could hold her and talk to her and look into her eyes.

I looked away from the doctor and gazed at my mother. She was asleep, but it was a fitful, agonized sleep. Even with all of the medication that she was receiving intravenously, Mom was moaning as if she were being tortured.

Dr. Ziegler took off her glasses. "Christy, Robert, we've known this was coming. . . ."

My dad's hands clamped down on my shoulders, as if he knew he wouldn't be able to stand without the support of my narrow frame. "We have known," he whispered, his voice full of anguish. "But somehow I don't think either of us believed she would ever really get this bad."

"I . . . I . . ." There were no words to express what I was feeling.

"You had better say your good-byes now," Dr. Ziegler continued. "There's simply nothing more we can do."

Dad nodded. He went to Mom's left side, then motioned for me to come stand next to him. "We'll say good-bye together," he announced.

With one hand I held on to my dad. With the other I reached out and held my mother's knee. "Mom?" I whispered. "Can you wake up now?"

She groaned in her sleep, but her eyes fluttered open. Since she had been in the hospital, a lot of the time, even when she was awake, her eyes had been cloudy from either pain or pain medication. But as she looked at us now, I could tell that she was lucid.

"Hi," she whispered. "Here are my two favorite people. Let's party."

"Oh, Rose." Dad's voice was barely above a

whisper, but he managed to smile as he leaned over to kiss her lightly on the lips.

Mom's eyes were full of gravity as she gazed at us. "I know what's happening," she said. "I can feel it."

Tears streamed down my cheeks, and I had to bite my lip to keep myself from starting to sob. "We're right here with you, Mom. We're not going anywhere."

She nodded. "I want both of you to know how much I love you," she whispered. "I've had the best husband and the best daughter that ever were. It's been a wonderful, fulfilling life."

"I love you, Mom," I told her. "You've been the best mother any girl could have. And you'll *always* be my mother—forever."

"Christy, please do one thing for me," she asked, her eyes filled with tears.

"Anything," I promised, my heart aching inside my chest.

"Remember that all I've ever wanted was your happiness," she told me. "Enjoy every moment of this precious life."

"I will, Mom. I promise." I was sobbing now. I couldn't stop the tears. I didn't even want to.

She turned to Dad. "Bobby, I want the same for you. Be happy. And take care of our little girl."

"I'll take care of her, Rose," Dad vowed, tears pouring from his eyes. He reached out and gently ran his fingers down her sunken cheek. "You can let go now, my love. We know you're tired. . . . Just rest."

170

As Dad and I clung to her, Mom closed her eyes. In a few seconds her breathing quieted . . . and then it stopped altogether. Beside us a monitor began to beep.

Dr. Ziegler stepped out of the shadows and switched off the monitor. "She's gone."

"Christy . . ." Dad let go of Mom and wrapped his arms around me.

I held tightly to my father, racked with grief. I could hear nothing but a sort of rushing in my ears, and my entire body throbbed with pain. Neither of us tried to hold back our sobs as we stood there, hugging and crying.

The time to be strong had passed. Mom was gone, and nothing would ever be the same again.

On Sunday morning I stumbled downstairs after a sleepless night. Dad and I had come home from the hospital together sometime after midnight. The house had seemed so empty that we had turned on every light. Then we had sat down together at the kitchen table, too tired to cry any more tears. It was almost dawn when we finally went to our rooms.

I had tried to sleep, but it was impossible. Memories had washed over me like, as they say, sands through an hourglass. Mom brushing her hair. Mom helping me pick out a new dress for the first day of second grade. Mom holding me on her lap while I cried because Craig Layborne was picking on me at school.

Sometime after dawn I finally processed the

truth. My mother had died. She was gone, and I would never see her again. I had thought I couldn't cry anymore, but I was wrong. I buried my face in my pillow and let out all of the emotions I had kept bottled up inside for the last few months.

When I had spent myself, I felt calmer. Along with the grief and the pain, I found myself feeling grateful that my mother's struggle was over. She was finally at peace.

I glanced at the phone in the hallway and thought about calling Jane and Nicole to give them the news. But no. I wasn't ready quite yet. I didn't want to say those terrible words aloud—not even to my two best friends.

Now I walked into the living room. This was the last place I had seen Mom before she had entered the hospital. She had been lying on the sofa, laughing and smiling as Dad snapped pictures of Jake and me.

I took a photo album from one of the shelves of our built-in bookcase and sat down on the couch in the exact spot where Mom had been. As soon as I opened the album, I felt transplanted in time, back to an age when my world had consisted of scraped knees, meat loaf, and naps.

The pages of the album were like chapters of my life. Mom had documented our lives on a constant basis. There were a dozen more photo albums on the shelves, and I knew that in the days leading up to the funeral, I would pore over each and every picture.

Looking at the images of my mother was painful, but I also found comfort in the sheer number of memories that we had captured on film. Years from now I would be able to sit down with my children and introduce them to their grandmother through these hundreds and hundreds of pictures.

"She'll never really be gone," I realized. Even now I could feel her presence around me, almost like a warm security blanket.

I flipped a page of the album. There was one of my all-time favorite pictures. It had been taken at my first birthday party. Molly Saunders stood off to one side, holding a one-year-old Jake. She was laughing as I, covered in birthday cake, reached up from my high chair and smeared Mom's face with pink frosting. Dad had told me that *he* had been laughing so hard, he had barely been able to focus the camera.

I reached out and touched my mother's cheek in the photograph. Then I slid the picture out of its plastic encasing. I was going to frame this one and keep it next to my bed, where I could look at it every morning and every night.

Lost in thought, I jumped when I realized that the doorbell was ringing. Part of me wanted to ignore whoever was at the door. But it wouldn't be right. There were other people who had loved Mom, and I knew they would want to share their grief with us on this terrible day.

I set the album aside and heaved myself off the

couch. There was only one person besides my dad that I *really* felt like seeing right now, and he was probably still asleep at this hour on a Sunday morning.

But when I opened the door, I found myself looking into Jake's eyes. I should have known. Jake had proved during the last few weeks that he would always be there when I needed him, and now here he was.

I could tell from the look in his eyes that his mother had given him the news. There was no need to say those dreaded words aloud.

"Christy . . . I'm so sorry." He took a step toward me, his face damp with tears.

I didn't speak. I simply succumbed to the magnetic pull I felt toward Jake. When I was close enough, he reached out and put his arms around me, holding me tight. As I had so many times recently, I allowed myself to let down my guard.

But these weren't the anguished, tortured tears I had cried this morning. These were tears of exhaustion and at relief at finding myself exactly where I needed to be. Even so, I was surprised by the sheer comfort I found in Jake's embrace.

"I'll be here as long as you need me," Jake promised.

I held him tight, feeling like I never wanted to let him go. *Maybe mother* does *always know best,* I thought. She had certainly been right about Jake. He was a special person . . . and he was my best friend.

Epilogue

A Few Months Later, Sometime at the End of August

"GRATED ZEST OF one lemon," I read aloud from the recipe for the springtime shrimp I was making. "Now what, exactly, is 'zest'?"

If Mom were still here, I could have called out to her and asked the question. It was an urge I still had twenty times a day. But now, over three months since her death, I didn't dissolve into tears every time I wanted to ask her a question or tell her a story or simply give her a hug and a kiss.

Sure, I still cried plenty. There were times when both my dad and I missed Mom so much that we would get in the car and go visit her grave just so we could tell her about how our days had gone.

But I had started to laugh again too. And when I wanted to feel close to my mother, I would head into

175

the kitchen to try out a new recipe. She had taught me to make my first pancake, and every time I mastered a new dish, I felt her presence, cheering me on.

And then there was Jake. It was hard to believe that several months ago I had considered him to be public enemy number one. We had been hanging out together all summer, just like we had when we were kids. We had ridden our bikes, gone out for pizza, watched movies, even revisited the diner where our friendship had fallen apart so many years ago. We had toasted each other with chocolate milk shakes (after carefully removing the ketchup bottle from the table) and vowed that we would never again let our pride stand in the way of what promised to be a lifelong friendship.

I hadn't called him an errant, onion-eyed bugbear even once. Times had changed, and even without Mom life had gone on—just like she had said it would.

With Jake I could talk about my mother without worrying that I was going to bring down everyone around me. Nicole and Jane had provided me with incredible support, but they hadn't known my mom when I was little. They didn't know the same stories that Jake did.

I ran a cheese grater over the rind of a lemon, hoping that I was right in assuming that this would provide me with the "zest" necessary for my recipe. If not . . . well, there was always another dish to try. It wasn't so much the product of my cooking that mattered, but the act itself.

Even Jake had said that he was starting to find cooking to be therapeutic. I had coerced him into making so many meals with me that he had actually begun to know his way around the kitchen.

Jake. Jake. For the past few weeks every thought I had that didn't involve my mother seemed to have one thing in common: *Jake.*

All summer we had been the best of friends. And that's what I had needed. Friendship, with no strings attached. But lately I hadn't been able to stop myself from thinking about *that* night. The night that Jake and I had been sitting on the sofa in his bedroom. The night we had been *this close* to kissing.

I set down the lemon and closed my eyes. In my mind I could see the look in Jake's eyes as he had leaned close. I could almost *feel* his full, red lips on mine. . . .

The fantasy ended abruptly when I heard the doorbell ring. I ran my hands under the faucet, then walked through the empty house to answer the door.

"Christy?" I heard Jake's voice from the other side of the door. "Are you in there?"

My heart began to pound as I opened the door. Jake stood on the front steps, holding a bouquet of wildflowers. Did the flowers *mean* something, or were they just a nice, *friendly* gesture?

"Hey!" I greeted him. "Want to help me make springtime shrimp?"

He grinned. "Actually, I had something else in mind—if the shrimp can wait."

"Okay . . ." I was confused but intrigued. Then I glanced over Jake's shoulder and saw a white limo parked at the curb, just as it had been on prom night.

"What's going on?" I asked. "I—I don't get it."

Jake bowed slightly from the waist. "If you'll do me the honor of accompanying me on a little journey, Christy, everything will become clear."

I took a quick mental inventory of the kitchen. The stove was off. The oven was off. The shrimp was in the freezer. There was nothing there that needed my immediate attention. "Sure . . . that sounds nice."

Jake looked incredible. He was wearing dark blue Levi's and a crisp white T-shirt that showed off his dark, golden tan. I, on the other hand, had flour in my hair.

"You look great," Jake said, his voice low. "Just perfect."

As he took my hand and led me toward the limousine, I felt like I had stepped back into my fantasy. Only this time maybe it was for real.

"Where are we *going?*" I asked forty-five minutes later. "Are you going to leave me in the middle of the forest and have me follow a trail of bread crumbs?"

The limo driver had dropped us off at a trail outside of town, and we had been walking into the woods for almost fifteen minutes.

He laughed. "Patience, my sweet. We're almost there."

My sweet. What a wonderful pair of words. I decided I didn't care where we were going. As long as I was with Jake, I was exactly where I wanted to be.

"Ta-da!" he announced a few minutes later. "We have arrived at our final destination."

My mouth dropped open, and I felt awash in pure delight. We had reached a beautiful, secluded spot in the forest . . . where Nicole and Justin and Jane and Max were sitting on a huge, red-and-white-checkered picnic blanket. Spread out in front of them was an elegant picnic supper. Nearby was a portable CD player and a huge pile of discs.

"This is amazing," I exclaimed. "But what are all of you doing here? What's going on?"

Nicole grinned. "We've all been feeling bummed that you never got to finish your senior prom," she explained. "So we're re-creating that magical night, right here, right now, our own way."

"It was all Jake's idea," Jane added. "He's been working for days to give you your own private 'prom' with all of your best friends."

Tears came to my eyes as I realized how much effort everyone, and especially Jake, had put into making this happen. But they were happy tears, for the first time in a long time. I was overwhelmed with emotion as I looked into Jake's twinkling blue eyes.

"I don't know what to say," I whispered. "Thank you."

He took both of my hands in his. "Just say that you'll have this dance with me . . . for your mom," he said quietly. "The next one will be for *us*."

Justin pushed play on the portable stereo, and suddenly the woods were filled with the sound of Frank Sinatra.

"I would love to dance with you," I told him.

Then I melted into his arms, and we began to move in the fading, dappled light. As I held Jake close, I felt surrounded by my mother's love. I was sure that she was watching us . . . and smiling.

But it wasn't just Mom's love that I felt. Suddenly I knew that I wasn't the only one who had been remembering the kiss that Jake and I almost shared. He had been thinking of it too. I felt his love as clearly as I heard the music.

As the last bars of the song ended, Jake drew me all the way into his arms. "Christy, this is something I've wanted to do for almost as long as I've been alive," he whispered.

And then my arms were around his neck, and our lips found each other. I felt like my entire being had opened up . . . like Sleeping Beauty when the prince awakens her with the soft touch of his lips.

The kiss deepened, and my body felt like it was on fire. I didn't care that my friends were watching. I was ready to kiss Jake in front of the whole world, if anyone was interested in watching. Deep down, this was a moment I had been waiting for as long as I could remember.

When at last Jake and I broke apart, I became aware that my friends were clapping and cheering. "Finally!" Nicole exclaimed. "I thought you two would *never* get together."

"We've found each other," Jake told Nicole. "In our own time."

"Yes, we certainly have," I agreed, staring into his eyes. "It took a long time, but it was well worth the wait."

I turned to my friends, who were beaming as if they had just won the lottery. "Thank you, everyone," I told them. "Being here, with all of you, it's easy to remember what really matters in life." I paused, gazing into Jake's eyes. "Family, friends . . . and love."

As another song began, Max pulled Jane to her feet, and Justin pulled Nicole to *her* feet. "Can we join the party?" Max asked.

"By all means!" Jake proclaimed. "This is our prom, after all."

I drifted back into Jake's arms as the rest of the group joined us on the "dance floor." This was a moment I would treasure for the rest of my life.

Again Jake kissed me, sending sparks up and down the length of my spine. I hugged him tight, feeling truly happy as I moved my eyes toward the sky.

You were right all along, Mom, I told her silently. *Mother* definitely *knows best.* Then Jake and I kissed again . . . and after that, the evening became a blur of laughing, hugging, and kissing. Just like Mom would have wanted.

Do you ever wonder about falling in love? About members of the opposite sex? Do you need a little friendly advice but have no one to turn to? Well, that's where we come in . . . Jenny and Jake. Send us those questions you're dying to ask, and we'll give you the straight scoop on life and love.

DEAR JAKE

Q: *I have a HUGE problem. My friends all tell me how obvious it is that my crush is crazy about me, but he still has not asked me out. I believe that some guys are too shy to ask girls out and I believe that sometimes girls have to make the first move, but I don't want to be rejected. How can I tell if he likes me or not?*

LP, Jasper, AL

A: When figuring out whether or not a guy likes you, you might want to consult this handy checklist:

Number One: Does he go out of his way to talk to you?

If I like a girl, I'll find any excuse to talk to her. I might even go so far as to start taking an interest in one of her hobbies.

Number Two: *Do all your friends tell you how obvious it is that he's crazy about you?*

Hello?!? Anybody home?!? You my friend, are one of the very few lucky ones because you already know that your object of affection likes you. Enjoy this rare and precious situation; take the ball and run with it. Make it easy on yourself by starting out with a casual suggestion to do something that's one on one, like going out for pizza or to a music store. You could also try the old "taking an interest in one of his hobbies" routine, and invite him to do something related. He will probably be flattered and relieved.

DEAR JENNY

Q: *I'm an Asian girl who's short and ugly. The guy I like is white, popular at school, and I heard that he doesn't go out with anybody. How can I get him to talk to me?*

YLV, Madison, WI

A: As long as you think of yourself as short and ugly, rather than the unique and wonderful person that you are, you are going to have difficulty getting to know anyone. You need to focus on your positive qualities rather than what you consider to be your negative qualities. Remember: there is nothing wrong with being short (or tall, or medium); beauty is on the inside; and anyone who wouldn't get to know someone based on that person's race isn't worth speaking to in the first place.

Do you have any questions about love?
Although we can't respond individually to your letters,
you just might find your questions answered in our column.
Write to:
Jenny Burgess or Jake Korman
c/o 17th Street Productions,
an Alloy Online, Inc. company.
33 West 17th Street
New York, NY 10011

Don't miss any of the books in *Love Stories*
—the romantic series from Bantam Books!